A Kat McGee Adventure
Book 4

Kristin Riddick

In This Together Media
New York

In This Together Media Edition, 2015

Copyright ©2014 by In This Together Media

All rights reserved. This is a work of fiction. Names, characters, places, and incidents either are the product of the author's imagination or are used fictitiously. Any resemblance to actual persons, living or dead, events, or locales is entirely coincidental.

Published in the United States by
In This Together Media, New York, 2015

www.inthistogethermedia.com

BISAC:

1. Girls & Women- Juvenile Fiction.

Cover Design and Illustrations by Nick Guarracino
Book Design by Steven W. Booth, www.GeniusBookServices.com

*To Moma and Grandmommy:
You made every Thanksgiving a feast of delectable smells
and tastes, but also taught me that kindness and gratitude
are just as important as homemade dressing and a good
buttermilk pecan pie.*

PROLOGUE

Dear Adventurers,

I'd personally like to welcome you to Kat's latest holiday tale. If you haven't met my granddaughter before, you are in for something special. If you have read about Kat's adventures in Treatsville, with Mrs. Claus and the School of Christmas Spirit, or her journey back in time with Thomas Jefferson and JQ Adams, you will notice something strange, or what I like to call *magical*, in this story.

Let me tell you why. These events all happened before Kat ever met Dolce, ate candy fruit, or saved the Declaration of Independence—this is Kat's very first holiday adventure. By the end of the book, you will understand why I chose to tell you about the other adventures first, and all will be explained . . . eventually.

Until then, enjoy. And thank you for coming along for the ride.

With love and magic,
Gram McGee

CHAPTER 1
THE TOTSVILLE FEAST AND GOBBLER GAMES

The thrill of victory. The agony of defeat.

Blood. Sweat. Tears.

The Olympics? Better.

The Hunger Games? Bigger. . . and without the hunting-for-your-life part.

These were the Gobbler Games—an event nine-year-old Kat McGee, the McGee family, and the entire town of Totsville, Maine, looked forward to all year. To prepare, Kat's six siblings, three brothers and three sisters, imposed intense training regimens on each other for months in advance: running, jumping jacks, push-ups, sit-ups, batting practice, kickball games, hide and seek, even freeze tag. Kat knew this was the year she wouldn't disappoint her family.

At least, that's what she hoped.

"Last again, Kat," her brother Ben teased as the McGees finished their morning family run. "That means you get to rake the leaves. We'll try to save some pancakes for you!"

Kat's father, Mac, handed her the rake and gave her an encouraging nudge as the rest of the family ran inside. "Almost there, Kat. We'll do some jumping jacks this afternoon to get the blood pumping again."

Kat managed a faint smile. Usually she hated tending to the yard, but today was different. Today, she didn't mind. Kat liked the sights and sounds of the crisp golden yellow, burnt orange, and deep red leaves piled in her yard on the first Saturday of Thanksgiving vacation.

As of today, they had less than a week left before Thanksgiving. Raking leaves gave Kat a break from the rigorous training program. It let her appreciate the smell of wood burning in fireplaces, the sounds of kettles whistling on stovetops, and the feel of a wonderful chill in the air on this bright and sunny fall morning.

Anticipation was in the air. The annual Totsville Thanksgiving Feast and Gobbler Games were about to kick off. Kat loved everything about this week—the smells, tastes, sounds, and sights of the town coming together to celebrate. Even with the intense competition, it was the one time of year when bickering siblings stopped fighting and feuding families shook hands. Everyone was in a good mood, and all the kids were friendly and kind to each other.

Which was not usually the case for Kat McGee.

For Kat, being different had become a way of life. Kat had long, unruly, curly hair that ponytails, braids, and barrettes could not seem to control. She was clumsy and often tripped, bumped, and bruised her way through the fourth grade at Totsville Elementary. Kat's awkward, somewhat insecure nature didn't help her chitchat or joke with her classmates. Plus, a shameful nickname from a not-to-be-talked-about accident in the first grade still haunted her three years later. All in all, Kat didn't have a lot of friends.

These differences may have made a more confident girl seem unique or quirky, but Kat thought she was ordinary. And in the McGee family, ordinary stood out—and not in a good way.

Kat's siblings were champions: students, athletes, musicians . . . each had ribbons and trophies and awards lining their walls to prove their prowess. Polly played violin, Ben swung golf clubs, Hannah made straight A's, Emily kicked her way through karate, Gus solved every puzzle given to him, and Abe knocked a high percentage of baseballs he hit out of the park.

But Kat, the quintessential middle child, had not found her one thing. She liked a lot of games, but she wasn't good at any of them. Her grades were mediocre, and she didn't find hobbies that stuck. Sure, Kat liked animals and television and apps, but she wasn't overly enthusiastic about (or obsessed with) video games or sports or . . . anything.

No, Kat McGee had only one major interest, and it was hard to quantify or reward. She knew anything and everything there was to know about . . . holidays. *All* holidays.

Kat loved Flag Day as much as Cinco de Mayo. She celebrated Chinese New Year, Martin Luther King Day, Christmas, Kwanzaa, *and* Chanukah. She made shamrocks on St. Patrick's, hearts on Valentine's, and hugged trees on Earth Day. Kat hopped around on Easter, paraded through town on the Fourth of July, and trick-or-treated better than anyone on Halloween.

But Thanksgiving, especially Thanksgiving in Totsville, was unlike any other holiday. Period.

Baked turkey. Deep-fried turkey. Turkey-in-a-bag. Brined turkey. Turducken. Cornbread stuffing, stuffing in-and-out-of the bird. Mashed potatoes, scalloped potatoes, and baked sweet potatoes. Boiled, baked, or casseroled green beans. Cranberry sauce, cranberry syrup, cranberry glazes. Giblet gravy, sausage gravy, lobster gravy. Pumpkin pie, Maine blueberry pie, buttermilk pie, pecan pie, rhubarb pie, and of course, whoopie pies . . . the list was endless.

The Totsville Thanksgiving Feast was so big it could literally stretch across the football field of Totsville High School, home of the Fighting Chickadees. Even though it was too cold to have the feast outside, Kat liked to imagine all the tables stretched from one end zone to the next, a gigantic chain of food and fun. But having the entire town form a huge horseshoe in the school gymnasium was also pretty cool.

Kat loved the table traditions at the feast. Many, like the new Mayor Leon Little's famous deep-fried turkey or Old Man Patterson's giblet gravy, were yummy standards, predictable and always good. In the McGee house it was Turkey Day Tamales.

As the town changed and grew, though, so did the table—and so did the feast.

When Kat's classmate Anjali Mehta's family had moved to town two years ago, they contributed a masala turkey and curried stuffing. Wow! Kat remembered the flavor explosion in her mouth when she tasted that bit of spicy goodness. Even though the Mehtas were relatively new to town, their dishes disappeared just as quickly as everyone else's.

The Kroloffs brought a different oyster dish every year—baked, fried, grilled, stuffed, or sautéed with vegetables. Mary Kim Vui's mom, who grew up in Vietnam, contributed homemade egg rolls.

The Swindles from Virginia introduced sauerkraut as a side dish. Kat had to admit that wasn't her favorite, but her brother Abe couldn't get enough of it. Mr. Swindle told Abe his appetite for sauerkraut was like that of a Hessian soldier in the Revolutionary War. As the youngest in the McGee clan, Abe beamed at the comparison.

Before the feast, the town of Totsville celebrated its history by recreating the voyage of the Totsville Ten-Forty, the train that had brought the earliest settlers to Totsville and established the town in 1842. The Ten-Forty had long been retired, but once a year, the Town Council cleaned it up, blew its whistle, and took the train on a journey through the state, following the trail of those early settlers.

Along the way, they stopped to gather food and supplies from all over Maine for the feast.

The council picked up pumpkin pies from Pie Parish, turkey from Turkey Township, corn from Corn County, fresh vegetables from Farmville, and shellfish from Oceanview, and then rode back into town to meet everyone in Town Square.

Every year Kat marveled at the train's great adventure. Kat sometimes complained to her mom that she never got to go anywhere or do anything exciting. Her mom would roll her eyes and send Kat off to read or do her homework. So Kat settled for watching the Ten-Forty roll into town, carrying the waving, happy Town Council and their bounty back to Totsville.

And then the games truly began.

Once the council returned, the next three days were a celebration of the pilgrimage—what was now known as the Gobbler Games. The town divided into two tribes, the Troubadours and the Tuckahoes. The two teams competed in a turkey race, a scavenger hunt, a pumpkin pie baking-then-eating contest, obstacle courses, dramatic reenactments and much more.

Finally, after the feast, the Thanksgiving celebration ended with a huge bonfire on Friday night. The winning tribe received a plaque with the families' names inscribed on it, a dedication on the Totsville Ten-Forty, and bragging rights for the rest of the year.

The McGees were Troubadours, through and through. Kat's grandparents were Troubadours, her great-grandparents were Troubadours—Kat knew nothing else. And because the

McGees were all very competitive, they would do almost anything to help the Troubadours win. With all the talent in the family, Kat had at least one sibling who was outstanding at every event.

Before Kat was born, the Troubadours had the longest winning streak—fourteen years—since the Gobbler Games had begun in the 1950s. But the tide had turned, and the Tuckahoes had won the last nine years in a row.

Kat was sure she had cursed the Troubadours. One year she tripped, fell, and brought Ben down with her during the three-legged race inches before the finish line. Last year she dropped an easy fly ball during the neighborhood softball game's final inning, and their squad lost to the Tuckahoes by one run.

So Kat tried and trained and thought that maybe this time she would make her family proud. Maybe this was the year she would break the curse.

CHAPTER 2
TROUBLE IN TOTSVILLE

"Someone has demolished the Ten-Forty! Hurry! We have to do something!"

Kat was startled out of her reverie by the sound of frantic screams. She turned and saw neighbors running down the street. Throwing on jackets, Kat's family streamed out of the house to join the crowd.

"What's going on?" Kat asked, seeing the worried look on her father's face.

"Come with us, Kat," her dad said, as Ben and Polly followed him to the car. "Everyone else, stay here and wait for news. We need to get to Town Square."

Kat dropped the rake and ran to the car. "What's wrong? What's happening?" she breathlessly asked Ben.

Ben shook his head as if to say, "Not now!" and threw on his seatbelt in the front. Polly and Kat crawled into the backseat, and Polly leaned over. In an urgent whisper, she said, "The council can't take the Ten-Forty on the pilgrimage."

Kat looked at her, confused. Polly shook her head. "The train, Kat. Someone's destroyed our train."

The Totsville Ten-Forty used to be the most famous train in all of Maine. People from as far away as Florida and California came to Totsville to see it.

The reenactments during the Gobbler Games had taught Kat and her siblings that a settlement had existed in Totsville for almost 200 years before the town was formally established; the village shared the land with the Penobscot, Maliseet, and Passamaquoddy Indians. But not until Maine became a state in 1820 did towns begin popping up all over the area. Once the Maine railroads were established in 1836, it wasn't long before Totsville officially became Totsville—an official town.

After bringing the earliest settlers, the Ten-Forty traveled across Maine so often for so many years that people said riding on it was like going back in time and being a part of history. But as years passed, people changed the way they wanted to travel.

By the 1950s, the decline of the United States railroad had begun, and it hit the Totsville Ten-Forty like a ton of bricks.

Travelers wanted to move more quickly and luxuriously. Passengers preferred airplanes and newer, faster trains. Train companies tried to remain competitive and made fewer stops to deliver hurried folks to their destinations. But eventually, the Ten-Forty lost its glory and was forced to retire. Kat had never even been able to ride on it.

Still, to the folks in Totsville, no new train could ever compare.

The train had collected many nicknames over the years—the Thanksgiving Turkey Train, the Gobbler Express, the Ten-Forty Furor. Some even claimed it was haunted.

The old Ten-Forty's restored and shiny locomotive, passenger car, and caboose—a smaller version of the original grand train—stood in Town Square, the epicenter of Totsville. To all who visited or lived there, it was an emblem of the early settlers' bravery.

And the townspeople kept the Ten-Forty alive by keeping the journey it took alive. The Ten-Forty couldn't run the way it did in its heyday, but the railroad commission still kept it in good enough shape to handle that one very important trip each year—the council's Thanksgiving week pilgrimage.

And now someone had ruined it all.

Kat thought it must be a joke. Why would anyone want to destroy the Ten-Forty?

Half of the McGee clan arrived at Town Square a few minutes later. A chaotic scene awaited them. News trucks from neighboring towns were scattered along the street, and a press conference had been called.

Some townspeople were crying. Some were hysterical. Some sat, looking worried and suspicious. Others ran around, not knowing what to do.

But everyone pointed and gasped at the wreck of a train in the center of it all.

Gone was the restored, shiny, beautiful relic of a bygone era that had welcomed hundreds of tourists and guests. Replacing it were disjointed pieces of steel, wood, and metal that looked more like a Lego project gone bad than a train.

The whistle was shattered. Only a torn scrap of metal remained. The space at the top of the locomotive, where the chimney normally blew smoke into the crisp autumn air, was now a piece of metal with more holes than a box of Cheerios. Windows were shattered. Broken boards, jagged pieces of metal, and bent rods and beams shot out in every direction like porcupine quills. So many parts and pieces were out of whack that the front of the car slumped forward, like a legless broken table thrown out at the dump.

Yellow police tape surrounded the Ten-Forty, which was now a crime scene. The crowd hushed as Mayor Little and Police Commissioner Pendergrass stepped to the microphone at the podium.

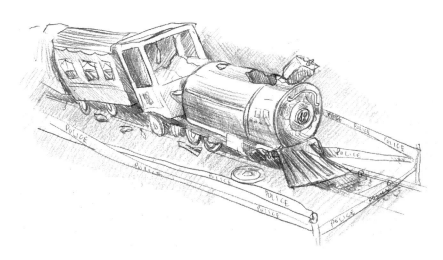

The commissioner spoke first. "Hi folks, and sorry for the disruption. We have a situation," he said, clearing his throat. "At approximately 4:36 this morning, we were alerted to a disturbance here in Town Square. Upon arrival, we saw what you now see behind us, the remnants of our Ten-Forty."

Murmurs spread through the crowd.

"The important thing is that no one was hurt," Mayor Little said, stepping forward.

"But the train! Look at it!"

"How will you take the trek?"

"What's the Town Council going to do?"

"Who would do this?"

Mayor Little quieted the crowd. "I know you have a lot of questions, but we ask you to leave things to our professional law enforcement. They have the situation under control. Please go back home. We will announce any news as soon as we have it."

"What about the feast? Thanksgiving is less than a week away!"

"How will we get the food?" A voice shouted from the crowd.

"And the Gobbler Games? What about them?"

Everyone looked at the mayor. He dropped his chin to his chest momentarily. When he looked back to the crowd, Kat knew things were bad.

Commissioner Pendergrass took over. "Unfortunately, the feast and the games are postponed until further notice," he said glumly. "Finding the perpetrators is our first priority. As you can see, several parts of the Ten-Forty are severely damaged. Some have been destroyed. And one, um, key part is missing."

Reporters shouted questions.

"What key part?"

"How much is the estimated cost of repair?"

"What all is missing?"

Townspeople murmured around Kat.

"Without a complete rebuilding of this train, and without the crucial missing piece, the council's trek is impossible," the commissioner lamented. "Until we find the responsible parties and they return this essential part, the Ten-Forty can not run. That's all I have for now."

Mayor Little and the commissioner answered none of the reporters' questions. As quickly as they arrived, they turned and walked back into Town Hall.

Thanksgiving without the feast? No Gobbler Games? Who would want to ruin Thanksgiving in Totsville? What is this missing part? Who would do something so terrible?

Kat's mind was flooded with questions. And her heart felt like it was broken. She wasn't alone. The normally festive, happy, and celebratory air in Totsville had vanished. Tension and accusations spread like wildfire. Everyone had a different theory; everyone proposed a different course of action.

Mr. O'Hara tried to get a group together to take on the police, saying they weren't doing their job fast enough. When

Mrs. Guerrero tried to reason with him, he muttered, "Don't be such a Troubadour."

And so it began.

At any other time of year, an outsider would never know the difference between a Troubadour and a Tuckahoe. They worked together, played together, and went to school together. They were neighbors, classmates, and friends.

Usually during the Gobbler Games, the competition between the Troubadours and Tuckahoes was fair and friendly. Every person and car wore or carried some bit of blue (Troubadours) or orange (Tuckahoes), and the spirit of the two tribes was everywhere. Banners, flags, and streamers adorned houses, shops, and restaurants.

Despite the competitive nature of the Gobbler Games, it was a community event, and the townspeople teased and chided each other playfully, with respect and admiration for the amount of dedication and loyalty in each tribe.

But with the train shattered and the feast and the games in question, the friendly competition was going south—fast. Attitudes soured. Fights broke out. People eyed their friends and neighbors with a suspicious glare.

The Scheins (Troubadours) sent Bernie Swindle (Tuckahoe) home after he gave their son Malachi a black eye. Malachi had accused Bernie of taking part in the crime. In turn, Mr. Swindle sent a nasty email detailing all of the things Mr. Schein had "borrowed" from him over the past two years and not returned.

Mrs. Gustafson cut off Mrs. Canales in the parking lot of the upscale clothing store Trendy Totsville.

Mr. Nez screamed at the bank teller, sweet old Mrs. Baker, for accidentally short-changing him a dollar.

The referee had to call off the Little League practice because parents and kids alike couldn't stop bickering.

Whispers blew through town like a threatening gust before a giant storm:

Maybe those Troubadours were trying to sabotage us!

I guarantee that Tuckahoe did it. Stanley has always been a bad influence on my Benji!

In a few short days, Totsville tore itself apart. It became a town divided. Neighbors and friends were now "that Tuckahoe" or a "typical Troubadour." By Monday morning, name-calling had escalated to profanity. Tiny annoying disputes became huge family feuds.

If someone didn't do something, Kat thought, Totsville would completely fall apart.

The McGee house was no different. Kat's parents were on edge, and the kids were arguing even more than usual. Emily yelled at Gus for taking her computer and jokingly changing the settings. Abe took all of Hannah's clothes from her closet and threw them on the floor for no reason whatsoever.

The town was a mess. The family was a bigger mess. And Kat was the biggest mess of all. Even hiding in her room in the corner of the fourth floor with her cats Salt and Pepper didn't help.

Kat knew someone had to find out who'd done this. Someone had to fix the Ten-Forty. If not, the feast wouldn't happen. The games would be canceled. And Thanksgiving, the most wonderful, comfortable, happy, yummy, fabulous family holiday of the year, would be ruined . . . taking the town of Totsville along with it.

That's when the doorbell rang.

CHAPTER 3
A MAGICAL MAP

"Surprise!" Gram McGee shouted as she dropped her bags and flew in the front door of the McGee house.

When no one ran to hug and kiss her or smother her with love, Gram knew something was terribly wrong. Kat usually barreled down the stairs when Gram arrived. Today, though, she simply walked downstairs and sat with her brothers and sisters on the couch.

And as Gram rounded the corner to the living room, she saw all her grandchildren—and their lackluster faces.

She frowned. Gram walked over to the television, shut it off, and took control.

"What's the problem here? Why the scowls? What's with the moping?"

Every room Gram McGee entered was instantly transformed into a place of light and fun and love. Gram was a spitfire who could ride a horse, drive a racecar, and bake any chef under the table. Since Kat could remember, she had wanted to be like Gram when she grew up. Gram lived in Seattle, but she always seemed to walk into the McGee house at precisely the right time.

While Gram loved all her grandchildren, Kat had always felt like they shared a special bond. Kat couldn't put her finger on what made her relationship with her grandmother so special, but it was as if they knew a secret language no one else understood.

"The Ten-Forty got trashed," whined Polly. Polly loved the Ten-Forty as much as Kat.

Emily plopped down on the couch. "And the feast and the games have been canceled—"

"Postponed," Marilyn McGee corrected from the kitchen doorway.

"Same thing," Hannah said sullenly to her mother.

"Well, that's not the way it should be at Thanksgiving, now is it?" Gram put her finger to her chin, as if she knew exactly what needed to be done. "We need to turn those frowns upside down! It's still Thanksgiving week, right? Think positively! Someone will fix the Ten-Forty. How bad can it be?"

Gram winked at Kat.

The McGee kids shrugged, but Kat nodded eagerly. She believed Gram. Gram always had something up her sleeve.

"What should we do?" Kat asked, coming to Gram's side. "Totsville's in trouble. We have to help."

"Oh please, Kat. Like there's anything *you* can do," Ben mumbled from the sofa. "You're the worst player in Gobbler Games history. What, you're gonna find the so-called missing link and put the train back together yourself?"

Hannah added, "You *are* still afraid of the dark, Kat."

Marilyn McGee shushed them. "No need to be ugly. But Kat dear, we should let the professionals handle it."

Gram looked at her grandchildren and shook her head. Then she grabbed her gigantic "Seattle: City of Goodwill" bag, closed her eyes, and started to move her lips. No sound came out, which was weird. But only Kat seemed to notice.

Five seconds later, Gram put the bag back on the floor and reached into it.

"Since you kids seem to be in such bad moods, I guess I'll have to take these back to Seattle," Gram said, setting six small bags on the floor in front of her. "And I guess my Turkey Day Tamales will go to the neighbors this year."

This at least got the McGee kids off the couch.

One: Who can resist presents from the greatest grandmother ever?

And two: Gram's Turkey Day Tamales were one of the best parts of Thanksgiving. She usually had to make a couple dozen extra, and was still forced to give each McGee a two-tamale limit before the feast to keep them from disappearing.

"Nobody make a mess," Gram warned as she handed out the gifts.

Polly and Emily got yo-yos that made noises when they went up and down. Abe got two baseball cards to add to his budding collection, and Gus opened a magic trick that he immediately took up to his room to investigate. Ben's gift of fluorescent golf balls actually provoked a smirk of appreciation.

Hannah received *An Old-Fashioned Thanksgiving* by Louisa May Alcott. Gram always said, "Start with the classics and you'll enjoy the new ones much more." As a thirteen-going-on-thirty-year-old, Hannah just rolled her eyes and tried to smile graciously.

As her siblings scattered about the living room and den to enjoy their new loot, Kat looked into her bag, excited. But then she pulled out what looked like a scroll with a piece of twine around it. Gazing up at Gram, she asked, "What is it?"

"You'll have to unroll it and see," said Gram. She knelt next to Kat and whispered, "There's always a way to help, Kat. Look closely. Only you can see where the tunnels will be. But you must believe."

Gram then stood up and straightened her dress, as if her quiet, mysterious exchange with Kat had never happened.

"I'm taking volunteers to help me with the tamales in ten minutes," she announced. She set her bags in the hall closet and walked into the kitchen with Kat's mother, shutting the swinging door behind her.

Kat ran up to her tiny room as fast as she could. Gram had given her a purple beanbag chair for her birthday. She sank into it, her present held tightly to her chest. Carefully, she untied the twine and unrolled the scroll.

Kat looked down at the wrinkled paper in dismay. A few words she had never seen before were scattered across the page, a star next to each one. Kat could make out drawings of trees, rocks, and a river; some other unrecognizable symbols were clumped together on different parts of the worn, old paper. A compass-like drawing in the corner showed north, south, east, and west.

"A map? She gave me a map?" Kat felt totally cheated. "What am I supposed to do with this?" she asked Salt and Pepper as they crawled across her legs.

Kat could hardly understand or pronounce the names—Zea Mays? Dyscordia? What did this have to do with the vandalism of the Ten-Forty? How would an old piece of paper bring Thanksgiving and the Gobbler Games back to Totsville?

Throwing her head back on her beanbag, Kat tossed the map onto the floor. *What did Gram mean?*

Kat closed her eyes and thought about what Gram had said: "Only you can see where the tunnels will be . . ."

An image of a creature made entirely of rocks popped into Kat's head.

"SSSffffssss . . ."

Kat's eyes snapped open. What was that sound? She looked from her window to the door. Both were closed. She laid back and closed her eyes again. Immediately, she saw a tall, curvy woman with indigo hands, a pink face, a white horn on her head, and a very long neck.

Her eyes popped open again. *What was that?!* Kat thought.

"Kkkkrrrrkkkk . . ."

Where are those sounds coming from? Kat scanned the room. Salt and Pepper both looked to Kat for reassurance. When Kat shrugged, they darted under the bed, instantly turning into scaredy cats.

Cautiously, Kat looked at the map she'd thrown on the floor. It was rolling up and un-scrolling on its own! Over and over. She checked the windows and doors—all closed. No breeze. No draft. How was this happening?

"SSSfffsss . . ." The scroll unrolled.

"Kkkkrrrrkkkk . . ." It rolled up again.

"OK. That's totally weird," Kat said aloud, even though she was the only person in the room. "Almost as weird as those things that popped into my head." She called out, "Gus, are you playing a trick on me?"

No answer.

She grabbed the map and studied it, hoping to see something, *anything* that looked familiar or would give her a clue about the Ten-Forty. She wanted so much to believe that the map was going to help Totsville.

As Kat looked more closely, something started to change. Her hands holding the ends of the scroll became warm. She closed her eyes again. This time she saw a map. It looked exactly like the map in her hands.

Each star on the map started pulsing, like beating hearts trying to jump off the page. Slowly, like an invisible hand sweeping a magic pen across the page, a dashed line connected the stars together. The resulting trail wound its way forward—and stopped at an X.

Kat opened her eyes. Sure enough, an X had appeared on her map, too! It was directly between the words "Zea Mays" and "Den of Dyscordia."

"Wow! How did that happen?" she exclaimed. "X marks the spot . . . like a treasure map! But what does the X mean?"

As if the map had heard her question, two sentences appeared next to the X: THE CODE KNOWS. KNOW THE CODE.

Code? What code? Kat thought.

POP!

POP! POP!

POP! POP! POP!

The sounds were popping off the map onto her lap and into her ears. Kat was dumbstruck. Answers to her thoughts appearing out of nowhere? Sounds coming out of a piece of paper? Was this a trick? What had Gram given her?

Kat turned the map over and saw little puffs of smoke popping off the back. When the smoke cleared, a jumble of letters, numbers, and symbols remained:

9:30:T-TT +; 10:35:TT-PP *; 11:15:PP-FV ^; 12:49: FV-T=

Beneath the random code was something that looked like an unfinished game of hangman or a *Wheel of Fortune* clue.

A _ _   A _ O A _ _ !

Kat jumped to her feet. She had an idea! She ran down the stairs and knocked on a door.

Nothing.

Then she remembered what day it was and knocked again—two long, three short.

The door cracked open. One of Gus's eyes peeked through the slit. On Mondays, Wednesdays, and Saturdays, he only opened his door in answer to a secret knock.

Kat's brother Gus could solve any puzzle. He won every board game the family played. He also loved magic, mysteries, languages, suspense, and practical jokes, so you never knew what you were going to get when you knocked on his door.

"State your purpose."

"Puzzle help," Kat replied.

"Proceed," Gus instructed.

Kat held up the part of the map with the letters and spaces.

It took Gus four seconds. "All aboard," he said. "Deposit fifty cents in the proper receptacle, *por favor*." Gus liked to practice expressing gratitude in multiple languages.

Kat dug a couple of quarters out of her pocket and slid them into a slot next to the doorknob. She heard the coins clink into a bucket on the other side.

All aboard! Kat thought, smiling and turning back to her room. *So it does have something to do with the Ten-Forty.*

But what? How is a map going to help fix it?

Then it hit her. If this map had something to do with the train, there was only one place in all of Totsville where she could find answers. Kat wondered if she should ask Gus to come with her in case there were more puzzles to solve. Or maybe Polly? Her sister was a train aficionada.

No. Kat shook her head. Even though she was nervous, she selfishly wanted to go by herself. If there was a treasure, shouldn't she be the one to find it? Gus and Polly didn't care as much about Thanksgiving as she did, anyway. And she'd been fighting with her siblings for two days straight. Why should she ask them?

Plus, Gram had given Kat the magical map, not any of her brothers or sisters.

It was hers. She'd go it alone. She didn't need their help. She just had to figure out how to sneak away to start her adventure.

CHAPTER 4
THE RESURRECTION OF THE TEN-FORTY

"Where do you think you're going, young lady?" boomed a voice from the back of the garage.

Kat stopped dead in her tracks. *Shoot a monkey*! She had almost made a clean getaway.

Gram walked out of the shadow, barely hiding a sly smile. "It's going to be dark soon, and your mom said the police chief told everyone to stay close to home." Luckily her voice sounded more concerned than angry.

Kat stammered, "I . . . um . . . wanted to run to the . . . " She couldn't think of a good enough lie. And she didn't want to lie to Gram.

"Did the map tell you what you wanted to know?" Gram asked, her mischievous smile now stretching across her face.

"Yes!" Kat shouted. She lowered her voice, but in her excitement her whisper wasn't that quiet. "What did you do to the map? I thought you'd made a mistake and given me a magic trick instead of Gus, but it was for me, right?"

Gram smiled. "Of course it was for you. Like I said, only you could see it."

Kat beamed. "But . . . how did you do that? Where did you get it? How does it work?"

"It came from a special place," Gram said with a wink, but then said no more.

Kat looked at her watch. "I'm not sure what it means, but if it will help Totsville, I'm going to the Ten-Forty to search for a clue. Maybe then the map will lead me somewhere else! Will you come with me, Gram?"

Gram didn't hesitate. She turned and grabbed Kat's mom's bike from the corner. "We have 37 minutes until we need to be back for dinner. If we're late, your dad will send out a search party. It's now or never."

Kat didn't know if she had ever loved her Gram more than at that moment.

For almost the entire year, the Ten-Forty stood in the center of Totsville's Town Square. The train's restoration was a big to-do in their town. The school had held bake sales and car washes, and the Town Council had sponsored fundraisers galore. Eventually, the old train looked almost as good as it had in its prime.

Scrubbed and polished, the locomotive, passenger car, and caboose looked magnificent. On display inside were maps, blueprints, newspaper articles, books, and original pieces of the train showed that the history of the Ten-Forty's tenure in Totsville. There wasn't anything flashy or fancy—the design and decor were simple and understated. But the minute they stepped inside, tourists learned the history of Totsville through the eyes of the Ten-Forty.

And then, once a year, the city employees transformed the Ten-Forty from a museum into a working locomotive, and the Town Council made the pilgrimage.

Not this year.

The emerging details of the Ten-Forty's demise were murky. The planned maintenance before the council was scheduled to leave went off without a hitch. But sometime between the maintenance check and the departure, less than twelve hours in all, the vandals struck. And now it was a mess.

Yellow police tape roped off the Ten-Forty's pieces. Kat felt like she could cry. It was worse than Humpty Dumpty.

Gram and Kat parked their bikes and headed to the train, not knowing if or how they would get inside.

A lone guard stood at the gate entrance. "You folks are supposed to be at home," he said. His grimace showed he meant business.

"I . . . ummm . . . I know, Herman," Kat stuttered, suddenly tongue-tied. "But this is my gram and . . . we wanted to see if . . . see, she just got into town . . . can we go inside? She's from Seattle."

Herman may not have noticed Kat's bumbling; his voice was stern. "I'm afraid I can't let you inside, Miss Kat. Strict orders. The police swept the area pretty good for prints and clues, but there may be evidence they missed. Besides, it could be dangerous."

Disaster. Luckily, Gram came to the rescue.

"I understand the predicament," Gram said. "*But I promise you won't know we were there.*"

When she looked at Herman and slowly emphasized the last words, Kat could have sworn she saw a sparkle in her grandmother's eye. Kat blinked, confused—then . . .

Shockingly, Herman's scowl softened and he nodded. "Five minutes is all I can give ya. Commissioner Pendergrass would have my hide if he knew I let anyone in."

"I'll drop off some turkey tamales this week in thanks," Gram said, smiling.

"Aw, ma'am, that'd be awfully kind of you," Herman smiled, tipping his hat to Gram.

Kat grabbed Gram's hand and pulled her up the steps. "We'll be out before you can say Ten-Forty!"

The train car was silent. Kat had never stepped onto the Ten-Forty without her whole third grade class or her entire family along for the ride. Being here with just Gram was eerily quiet.

And the Ten-Forty was a *mess*.

Books were scattered on the floor. The photos and newspaper clippings that normally lined the walls were broken or stacked in boxes, ready to be moved to make way for a trek that wasn't going to happen.

"What should I be looking for?" Kat cried, distraught. "I'm never going to find out what this map is supposed to mean in five minutes! This place is a pigsty!"

"Always worried about the time. Well, maybe that will help you," Gram said, cryptically, glancing at the map in Kat's hands. She turned, surveying the space. "You know what? I think I'll keep Herman company while you figure it out."

With that, Gram stepped toward the door.

"What?!" Kat exclaimed. "No! Gram, I need your help! Herman won't like it if you leave me in here alone."

"You're a big girl, Kool Kat." Gram said. "Let me worry about Herman." She looked at the map and nodded. "Look. Listen. And learn."

Gram smiled, stepped off of the train and closed the door.

What?! Kat thought. She frantically looked around the small space.

At the top of one box, a broken, wood-framed, yellowed newspaper article read, "Totsville Ten-Forty First Train to Cross Maine."

Photos of happy Totsvillians boarding the train in the 1940s smiled out from another box. Kat saw books, stacked in piles, with titles like *A Train History of Maine*, *The Totsville Ten-Forty's Centennial*, *A Train and a Town*, and *A Thanksgiving History in Totsville*.

Shattered glass enclosed a drawing depicting one of the most famous historic events in Totsville. Shards of the glass littered the floor. Kat picked up the splintered frame and saw the drawing of writer and magazine editor Sarah Hale's rumored visit to Totsville in 1862.

By the age of five, every Totsvillian knew of Sarah Hale. After 17 years spent trying to convince presidents of Thanksgiving's significance, Sarah Hale continued to lobby President Abraham Lincoln, who finally made Thanksgiving a national holiday in 1863. To have such a famous person visit to the budding town of Totsville was legendary. The plaque given at the end of the Gobbler Games was even called Hale's Halo. How could someone destroy such a town treasure?

Still, Kat didn't know how any of this history of Totsville and the train would help her. She opened a couple of books with the very tip of her finger, careful not to move or alter anything. But she had no idea what she was looking for, and most of these books were too hard for her to read, anyway.

Defeated, Kat closed her eyes.

Again, she saw the tall, curvy woman with indigo hands, a pink face, a white horn on her head, and a very long neck. *Not again*, Kat thought, opening her eyes. *Who is that? Why do I keep seeing her? What's wrong with me?*

Kat pulled the map from her backpack and unrolled it. Again, her hands felt warm. Again, she looked at the unfamiliar words: Zea Mays, Den of Dyscordia, Trolltropolis. She focused on the X and the statements next to it: "THE CODE KNOWS. KNOW THE CODE."

Click click.

Kat's head shot up. The door in front of her, to the control room, had a very large sign on it that read, "KEEP OUT: AUTHORIZED PERSONNEL ONLY." But the small brass handle to slide the door open was clicking, like it was trying to open but had gotten stuck.

Click click.

Click click.

Kat glanced out the window and saw Herman chuckling. Gram must be entertaining him with one of her many funny stories. "It's now or never," Gram had said. Kat knew it was her turn.

Taking a deep breath, she walked to the door and put her hand on the brass handle.

"Ouch!" she yelled. The handle was burning hot.

But as Kat jerked her hand away, the door slid slowly open. It was too dark to see what lay beyond. She felt her heart pounding. *What could it be?* Kat thought.

Kat cautiously stepped into the room, and the door slid shut behind her.

Wow.

Once the door closed, she saw that the room was aglow. This small compartment was nothing like the demolished car Kat had just left. Nor was it the clean and shiny Ten-Forty she was used to seeing. This place looked . . . old. Dusty, dirty knobs, levers, buttons, cranks, gauges, numbers, and charts littered the tiny compartment.

Kat had stepped into the brain of the train: the conductor's cab. Somehow, it had escaped the destruction and vandalism . . . except for one thing.

Of all the knobs and flips and switches, police tape surrounded only one part of the mechanisms—the throttle, which Kat knew was how the train moved. Kat looked closer. On top of the throttle was a keyhole. Kat blinked. She'd never heard of a throttle having or needing a key. And this was not your average keyhole. It was huge! It was almost as big as the throttle itself.

Kat leaned closer and squinted into the gaping hole. She couldn't see anything. *Maybe this is what's missing?* Kat thought. *Maybe this is why they can't fix the train!*

Impulsively, Kat stood up and turned the map over. She looked at the jumble of numbers, letters, and symbols that had mysteriously popped up in puffs of smoke earlier:

9:30:T-TT +; 10:35:TT-PP *; 11:15:PP-FV ^; 12:49: FV-T =

Then she looked at the panel of gauges and knobs and levers, and she blew away the dust and cobwebs.

Oh boy.

She looked at the code again. Something about it seemed familiar.

Wait a minute!

Kat had just seen this code!

She turned and tapped the handle to the sliding door to make sure it wasn't hot. When she felt it was cool again, Kat tried to slide it open.

It was locked.

She didn't have time to struggle—she had to go with her gut.

Kat turned back to the control panel and looked again at the code on the map. Could the code be a train schedule? The pile of schedules in the other car listed times and places that the Ten-Forty had traveled. And the schedules beside the newspaper clippings had looked a lot like this:

9:30: Totsville to Turkey Town; 10:35: Turkey Town to Pie Parish.

If only she could go back and check.

But this had to be it! T for Totsville, TT for Turkey Town, PP for Pie Parish—all the places the train used to run! It made complete sense.

Kat spread out the coded map in front of her. A punchboard panel with times and station codes sat to her right. She pushed in the line of code on her map—9:30:T-TT +; 10:35:TT-PP *; 11:15:PP-FV ^; 12:49: FV-T= exactly as it appeared.

Nothing happened.

Ugh! I must need a key! Deflated, Kat looked down at the gaping hole in the throttle. Gram and Herman would return for her at any moment. She knew she shouldn't, but she stuck her fingers down into the space. Maybe the key was broken or a clue had been hidden inside—

That's when the throttle's metal morphed, melted, and covered Kat's hand like a rubber glove. She yelped, yanked, and tugged, but her hand was stuck! Then, the small compartment started to shake violently. Kat was thrown back into the conductor's chair, her hand still stuck inside the throttle. The panel in front of her lit up, the knobs turned, and the gauges sprung to action.

The train had come to life.

"What have I done?" Kat shouted. "Help! Gram? Herman? Help! My hand is stuck! I can't get out!"

Kat tried to stand, but the throttle-glove squeezed her hand more tightly and yanked her back into the seat.

And then, out of nowhere, came a woman's voice. "Welcome to the Ten-Forty! We hope you enjoy your journey. Next stop, Tunnels of Tutkium!"

That's when Kat McGee, for the first time in her nine-year-old life, fainted.

CHAPTER 5
INTO THE TUNNELS OF TUTKIUM

Kat was jolted awake by a sudden drop in her stomach—the same feeling she got when she rode the rollercoaster at Magic Isles in Thrillville, a few miles south of town.

In front of her, a control panel whirred. The needles on the gauges swished, the lights on the board blinked, and the knobs turned circles. Kat looked at her right hand. She felt a weird tingling sensation in her fingertips. Then she looked at the throttle. The police tape was gone, but the gaping keyhole in the center remained.

Did I dream that the throttle sucked in my hand and wouldn't let go? Am I still in the Ten-Forty . . . and is it moving?! *Wait, the Ten-Forty is alive! I have to get Gram in here.*

But when Kat looked out the window of the train, she didn't see Gram. Or Herman. All she saw was a blue sky and white clouds.

"Holy smokes! This train isn't moving . . . it's flying!" Kat screamed. Then she remembered that no one was there to hear her.

Where am I? How long was I asleep? How is this flying and where am I going? Kat was scared, but it wasn't all bad. She felt a nervous kind of excitement in her belly, too.

Grabbing her backpack, she spread the map Gram had given her across the control panel. Instantly, she felt a little better. *Gram told me to believe. Gram gave me the map. Surely Gram knows where I'm going. Maybe this will help me fix the Ten-Forty and bring Thanksgiving back to Totsville!*

The X on the map began to pulse, and a red light flashed in front of her.

Plus, Kat realized, *I'm finally on the Totsville Ten-Forty! And I'm flying!*

The woman's voice suddenly announced, "Now approaching the Tunnels of Tutkium! Please gather your belongings and prepare to exit. Thank you for traveling on the Totsville Ten-Forty, and please come see us again."

Wait a minute! Kat blinked, remembering that the same voice had spoken just before she fainted. *Tunnels of what? I thought we were going to Turkey Town! But I punched in the schedule code for Turkey Town! Where are the tunnels?*

As if in answer to Kat's thoughts, the train plunged downward in a nosedive through the clouds. Kat grabbed on to the arms of the conductor's chair, fastened the old-fashioned, rusty seatbelt so she wouldn't fly out of the seat, and pushed her feet into a cubby below the control panel because they didn't quite reach the floor.

Kat closed her eyes tight, hoping the train was not about to crash.

Shouldn't we be slowing down, not speeding up? Kat didn't know whether to squeeze her eyes shut or open them as widely as she could. They were heading straight for the ground . . . at full speed ahead!

Closer. Closer. Faster. Closer. Faster.

They were going to crash right into the ground!

I'm going to die and I'm only nine! Kat thought. *And I've never even been to Disney World!*

Kat couldn't watch anymore. She squeezed her eyes shut.

BOOM! CRASH! WHOOOOOSH!

Kat gulped.

The Ten-Forty had arrived.

Oh-so-slowly Kat opened her eyes. No flames billowing out of a crashed flying train. No broken bones—not even a scratch!

Holy moly! Did that really just happen? Kat felt amazed.

She grabbed the map and saw the X in the top corner had turned bright red. Instead of "KNOW THE CODE. THE CODE KNOWS," two new sentences had appeared next to the X:

"THE KEY TO THANKSGIVING GETS YOUR TRAIN BACK ON TRACK. THREE IS THE MAGIC NUMBER TO FIND YOUR WAY BACK."

The key to Thanksgiving? What was that supposed to mean? How would that fix the Ten-Forty? Three what?

She had to get out of the train and find some help.

Kat rolled the map up and shoved it into her backpack. Again, she tapped the door handle. Now it was no longer burning hot; it was freezing cold! When she let go, her hand was wet.

But the door slid open.

Instead of a disheveled train car full of boxes and articles and Ten-Forty paraphernalia, the room in front of Kat was empty. Nothing in it at all.

"Oh boy," Kat gulped. "I'm going to be in big trouble with Herman now."

More importantly, Kat realized, the three steps to the ground didn't lead anywhere near Town Square in Totsville. In fact, Kat wasn't even above ground. She looked around, shivering a little from fear.

Dirt. Darkness. Rock. Above, below, and around her. Nothing else.

Carefully, Kat stepped onto the damp, soft ground of what appeared to be a cave. From the outside, the Ten-Forty looked even worse than it had back in Totsville. It looked like it would never move again.

Glancing up, Kat saw a tunnel, but it was too dark to make out where it went.

What is going on?! Kat was starting to freak out. *How far underground did I go? How am I ever going to get out of here?*

Trying not to cry, she yelled out, "Gram? Herman? ANYONE? Somebody help me!"

Not knowing what else to do, Kat sat on the train's stairs. She put her head in her hands, closed her eyes, and took a huge breath. *What am I supposed to do now?*

She opened her eyes and looked at the ground.

On the wet dirt were railroad ties. The long blocks of wood extended out in front of her, but there were no train tracks attached. It looked like someone had forgotten to finish the job. But as Kat now knew, the Ten-Forty didn't need tracks anyway.

A dim light flashed in the distance, like a tiny flashlight or a faraway boat. Kat stood up. "Hello? Is somebody there?" The light was coming from another tunnel. When Kat turned, she saw that she had landed in the center of many tunnels, extending like the silk arms of a massive spider's web.

A very faint sound was coming from the tunnel with the light, but Kat couldn't recognize any words.

"Hooooooo kahhhhhh meeeeeee!"

Kat sighed, relieved. Maybe someone was coming to help. But then she got scared again. What if the person was coming to hurt her?

The closer and brighter the light became, the more Kat could see that the holder of the light was bouncing or jumping in the darkness. But she still couldn't tell if it was a person or an animal or a thing or a creature or an alien.

Kat decided to chance it and call out again. It was better than being alone. "I can't hear you!"

"Hold on, Kat Meeee!" The sound echoed through the tunnel.

"OK, sounds like a person, but did that person say my name?" Kat whispered to herself.

"Yes! I am coming to help you Kat McGee!"

A man's voice, definitely. But how could he have heard her? She'd only whispered!

The light came closer and closer. Kat stood and hesitantly took a few steps forward.

It was indeed a man, and he was having quite a hard time. He bent down as if to rest and catch his breath. Kat wished that she had her brother Ben's night vision goggles so she could see what he was doing, but she'd find out soon enough—he was coming straight down the tunnel toward her.

Should I run the other way or stay put? Kat couldn't decide. Could he help her or was he going to bury her alive? Maybe he'd feed her to a pack of angry cave monsters. Who knew?

Kat took out the map and the only other thing she had in her backpack, a Fighting Chickadees pencil, and stood at the ready. Just in case she had to fight . . . or run for her life.

But as the man came into focus, Kat's fear started to dissipate. The man was jumping from railroad tie to railroad tie, laughing every time he couldn't make it, which was most of the time. Every few feet he had to stop, put his hands on his knees, and rest, huffing and puffing. He would then stand and continue merrily along, skipping down the ties. His laughter echoed down the tunnel toward Kat.

Finally Kat could see him clearly, and he had the biggest smile Kat had ever seen. His chuckles were more like a jolly schoolboy's than those of a wrinkled, older man. *He looks older than Gram, but he smiles as much as she does!* Kat thought. The resemblance made her smile, too.

The man was chubby, and his dark-skinned cheeks and forehead glistened with sweat. He wore an oversize V-neck poncho shirt with beaded trim, and his black jeans seemed too long and baggy for his short, squat body. His dark hair was straight and thick, and bobbed up and down when he skipped, like it was moving in slow motion.

Kat was still wary; this jovial Native American grandfather was still a stranger. And Kat knew to be wary of strangers, regardless of how friendly they seemed.

But as soon as he spoke, that reticence disappeared as well.

"Kat McGee! Tan khak! You are early! Your gram told me not to expect you for many more minutes, but I am glad you are here now!" The man spoke in excited exclamations, as if he was greeting a long-lost cousin. And he did it all with that same huge smile on his face. "Welcome to the Tunnels of Tutkium!"

Kat smiled on the inside but kept her cool on the outside. "How do you know my name? And how do you know my gram? What's your name? And how far underground are we? I thought I was going to Turkey Town—how did I get here?"

"So many questions, young one!" The man chuckled again. "Perhaps I call you *espons*, for they are curious too!"

Kat stepped back. "Excuse me? What is an ez punz?" Kat said defensively. "Is it bad? And what does tawn gok mean? Are you speaking English?"

The man chuckled again. "Apologies! Yes, I speak English and the language of my people, the Malimaquiddies, too. *Espons* is what you call a raccoon—a very curious creature that I like very much. And my name is Mitsu. It means 'eat' in your language." He patted his belly and giggled. "As you can see, I like eating very much!"

Kat couldn't help but smile, though she wasn't sure she liked being compared to a raccoon. Mitsu was like the Jolly

Green Giant, without the green and giant part. How could she not like him?

"Very nice to meet you, Mitsu. Should I say tan khak too? We have Passamaquoddy and Maliseet tribes in Maine. Are the Malimaquiddies related?"

"Kat McGee! I knew you were smart! Yes, those tribes are relatives—what you call cousins—to the Malimaquiddies. And *tan khak* is a greeting . . . like hello! Or welcome! I will teach more as we go! We need to find something for you, yes?" Mitsu turned as if to leave.

"How did you know?" Kat asked, momentarily forgetting her suspicions.

Mitsu paused and smiled. "I know many things about you Kat McGee. We will get to each one in its turn, but now we must go." His smile faded for the first time and his eyes got a glazed, distant look. "I know your time is short."

The air chilled. Kat shivered. "You're not leaving me alone, are you?" she asked nervously, running toward him.

Mitsu snapped out of his trance and looked at Kat quizzically. "Why, of course not! That is why your gram sent for me! To help you through our world! She knows what has happened to the Tunnels of Tutkium."

Kat sighed. "Whew!" But then Mitsu's words registered, and Kat frowned, perplexed. "Wait, Gram has been here? In the Tunnels of . . ." She hesitated. She couldn't even say it. "Tootkeeyum?"

Mitsu smiled. "That is a good try! Tutkium means 'peace' in your language. We are a world beneath your world. The tunnels of peace were created between my people and the other beings that inhabit this underground world. The humans, creatures, and spirits used to travel freely, going from our home to other kingdoms, and all through the tunnels," he said, motioning around them.

Kat peered into the dark passageways but had a hard time picturing what lay ahead. "You mean like highways or interstates?"

It sort of made sense: Kat had been on a few family camping trips to see the balsam fir, black spruce, and white cedar trees in the North Maine Woods, but she had never taken a highway to a totally different land. Kat imagined the sunny beaches of California down one tunnel, or Disney World down another! Cool!

"Ha! Yes! Much like that! The tunnels used to connect our lands and people, but it is different now. Tutkium has changed since your gram was here!"

Kat felt a small sense of relief that Gram had been to Tutkium as well. But then it dawned on her. "Hold on a sec. If Gram has been here, and I came on a flying train, then Gram *must* know magic! I mean, if she came here and sent me here, right? Are you magic, too?" Kat's mind was racing with questions.

Mitsu chuckled. "Ah, *espons*, magic is tricky, but—"

The ground began to tremble, interrupting him. Kat grabbed his arm.

"Wh— what's happening?" she whispered, afraid that speaking up would make the ground shake again.

Mitsu's smile faded. "We must go, before Dyscordia discovers us. She feels your goodness and our budding friendship. She will come quickly."

Kat instantly recognized the name. *Den of Dyscordia.* She unrolled the map in her hand, and pointed to the spot. "This Dyscordia?"

Mitsu grabbed the map and held it up, like he had just won a trophy. "Your gram! Your gram is very clever." Then Mitsu read the instructions on the map aloud,

> "THE KEY TO THANKSGIVING GETS YOUR TRAIN BACK ON TRACK. THREE IS THE MAGIC NUMBER TO FIND YOUR WAY BACK."

He nodded and smiled. "I think I know what this map means."

Kat was astounded. "Do you know where to find the key to Thanksgiving? Is it an actual key? Or is the key not supposed to be a real key but—" She couldn't remember the word.

"A figurative key?" Mitsu asked.

"Right, right," Kat said. "Figurative is something like a symbol, right?" Mitsu nodded. "But if it's not a real key we're looking for, how do we find something that isn't real? And how will something that isn't real help fix the train? Because it looks to me like the throttle is missing one mighty large key, not three."

Kat pointed her thumb behind her to the conductor's cab.

Mitsu shined his light into the darkness in the direction she was pointing, and his face brightened.

"Well if it isn't the old Ten-Forty! I wondered if it was running again! Looking a little worse for the wear, yes? But still, the Ten-Forty will help us move quickly!"

Kat was shocked. "You know the Ten-Forty?"

"Of course! How do you think your gram traveled here?" Mitsu was already climbing the stairs to the Ten-Forty's cab. He urged Kat to hurry and follow him.

Mitsu did not even touch the hot/cold handle. He simply waved his hand in front of the door, and silently it slid open. Mitsu perched himself atop the conductor's chair as if he'd done so a thousand times. He placed the map in front of Kat and asked her to keep watch over it—he would need her help soon. He then looked at the throttle. His eyes widened.

"It is as I suspected." He looked at Kat. "You are right, Kat McGee. This train needs a very special key." Mitsu pointed at the empty keyhole in the throttle. "The Ten-Forty needs the Tutkium Talisman. Without it, the train cannot run in your world."

Kat was excited—finally, a clue!

"OK. So do you know where this Talisman is? How do we get it?"

Mitsu shook his head. "I'm afraid the Talisman has been hidden, maybe even destroyed. Dyscordia stole it. Only she knows where the Talisman is. But this map may give us clues. I believe that is why the map tells us the magic number of three." Mitsu pointed at the other blinking dots on the map. "Three places, three clues!"

"Great! Let's get going!" Kat said, excited they had a plan.

For the first time, Kat saw what she thought was fear in Mitsu's eyes. "But the clues may also lead us to Dyscordia."

Kat shivered. All around them, the ground shook even more violently.

"There is no time to waste. I will explain more, but first we must get out of here. It's too dangerous to stay."

Mitsu immediately went to work pushing buttons and pulling levers. Once again, the train roared to life, but not with the sound of a traditional train on tracks. Instead, Kat felt it creak, crackle, and squeak its way off the ground.

"Stay with me, old friend!" Mitsu said, patting the controls like an obedient dog.

Sitting beside Mitsu, Kat felt her mind reeling from everything he had told her about Gram, Dyscordia, the tunnels . . . She wanted to know so much more!

But before she could open her mouth, Mitsu pressed a button. He smiled at the sound of the announcer's voice. It was the same sweet but strong voice Kat had heard twice now. This time the voice bellowed, "All aboard! Next stop, Trolltropolis!"

"Trolltropolis? As in t-t-trolls?" Kat stammered. She'd seen the dot on the map, but had hoped to avoid it. "I don't suppose they're cute and cuddly trolls, are they?"

"Kat McGee! Don't worry!" Mitsu looked at Kat, whose eyes showed fear, curiosity, and confusion all at once. He took Kat's hand and placed it between his two warm palms. "We are now friends! I will protect you! And all your questions will be answered."

Kat thought of a lot of things that could be worrisome, even dangerous. But when she looked at Mitsu's sunny smile and kind eyes, she felt safe, like she did with Gram. She believed him. And what was the other option? Go into those tunnels alone? Thank you, no!

So as the Ten-Forty magnificently and magically lunged forward into the deep, dark, cavernous tunnel, Kat McGee did not faint—she enjoyed the ride.

The edges of the woman's long, dark crimson cape dragged over the floor of the cool cave as she paced back and forth. Distant screams and shouting drifted in and out, wafting through the tiny tunnels like a bickering breeze.

A pool of water on the floor glowed brightly, a faint picture of a man and a little girl shining on its surface.

"Enough!" the woman shouted. The light and picture disappeared, leaving the water dark and still again.

"Tsk, tsk, tsk," she said, her deep voice echoing off the walls of the cave. "The old man has most definitely lost it. He thinks it will be easy to defeat me. With that child no less!"

She turned to the tiny tunnels and stretched out her arms toward the openings in the cave. Her long, antennae-like steel fingernails stretched out and curved toward the holes, like bent lightning rods, each one directed toward an opening in the cave's wall.

"Give me your strength," the woman commanded.

The distant screams and shouts grew louder. Bolts of midnight blue light spurted from the crevices in the cave, summoned to the woman's fingers like iron to magnets. The light caught her steel fingertips, rolled up her arms, and flashed through her body, which seemed to glow with renewed energy. Even her hair, a mass of midnight blue that twisted and turned to form what looked like a pile of snakes, glowed warmly.

The woman opened her eyes, which flared with a matching midnight blue light. Abruptly, she turned and snapped. "Malsom, come here."

A dark-as-night wolf ambled over to the woman. She stroked its head.

"We must prepare. You know how I feel about visitors."

Kat McGee and The Thanksgiving Turkey Train

CHAPTER 6
THE POOKCHEENSQUAS'S PURSUIT

"The Tunnels of Tutkium were filled with joy! We Malimaquiddies kept to ourselves for the first thousand or so years we lived here. But at last, our people decided to explore the Tunnels of Tutkium.

And we discovered many fascinating lands.

Each one—be it a world for creature, human, spirit, or animal—was more intriguing than the last. We befriended the inhabitants, and we all brought something different to our world beneath your world: food, customs, ceremonies, culture, magic! We learned from each other and shared everything."

Mitsu stared off into the tunnels, remembering a better time.

The dips and turns of the train made Kat feel as if she was floating down a slow and steady river and hitting a few rapids along the way. Mitsu guided the train like a symphony conductor, swaying and waving his hands to music only he heard.

Mitsu's smile faded as he continued, "But Dyscordia is a creature like no other. She can only live and breathe and exist when surrounded by chaos."

"What do you mean?" Kat asked, confused. "She can only survive if people are fighting?"

"Yes, Kat McGee! Dyscordia needs negative energy to grow powerful. It is what keeps her alive. Once she finds that negativity, she absorbs it and gets stronger. She grew until she was strong enough to create the chaos herself."

Mitsu shook his head. "She caused misunderstandings among our people. They escalated into huge feuds. Soon they spread between our people and the trolls, then to all animals and creatures in our land—everyone and everything fought. The lands separated. The people dug more tunnels. They escaped our community to live separately. Some built walls. Some used other means to keep away those who were unlike them.

"That's why you saw no one when you arrived. There is no more Tutkium, only *modocs*—what you would call enemies. Dyscordia spreads the chaos to make herself stronger. Now everyone is scared of her, and of each other. They are scared of what she can do."

Kat didn't like the sound of this Dyscordia character one bit. Not only did she seem scary, but she also sounded meaner than Julio, the fifth grade bully who beat up kids for their lunches. Kat didn't know if she should be more afraid or angry, but she wanted to know more. "Where did she come from? Why does she want everyone to fight?"

Mitsu smiled again. "Kat McGee! I ask the same question all the time! Peace destroys Dyscordia. She was born from a spark of turmoil, and she knows only what gave her life—and that is chaos, anger, and fear. But do not ever call her a witch. She will turn your ears into corn cobs!"

Kat snickered at the image but quickly stopped when she realized Mitsu was serious.

"If she isn't a witch," Kat asked, "what is she?"

Mitsu leaned toward Kat and whispered, "In my land we call her Pookcheensquas."

"Bookcheen-what?" Kat had never heard of such a thing! And how does a thing come from a *spark of turmoil*? She was so confused.

"Pookcheensquas. Because she abuses magic, and knows not how to use it for good."

Ahhh, the magic again! *Everyone down here must be magical.*

But this kind of magic didn't sound like the kind that had helped Kat travel to the Tunnels of Tutkium. Kat studied Mitsu. When he talked about Dyscordia, his face changed from silly and smiling to fearful and cautious. Kat was beginning to see this Pookcheensquas was nothing but trouble, and she felt frightened but still curious.

"What kind of magic does she use?" she blurted out. "Was she created from evil magic? How did she make people hate each other? Did she put them under a spell? Did she force them to drink purple poisonous smoking liquid that smelled like toads?"

Mitsu chuckled. "Ah, young *espons*! Such imagination! Dyscordia preys on fear! She uses trickery to make people afraid of what they don't know. She makes them feel insecure, so that they think everyone else is an enemy! Most have not been strong enough to fight her! It takes a lot of things to be immune to her spells, but we believe you have those qualities, Kat McGee!"

Kat's jaw dropped. "Me? How am I supposed to help?"

Mitsu looked at her. "We must stop the chaos before she can destroy your world the way she has destroyed ours."

Kat's eyes widened. "My world?"

Then it hit her. Mitsu's description of Tutkium sounded a lot like her hometown. The Totsville she'd left behind, after the vandalism of the Ten-Forty, was full of fighting families and friends. There was more anger and ill will there than Kat had ever seen—she couldn't believe how quickly it had gone downhill. It had seemed almost . . . impossible.

"Dyscordia destroyed the Ten-Forty," Kat guessed.

Mitsu's look told her she was right.

"She's trying to do to Totsville what she did here. She's trying to make everyone hate each other." Kat couldn't believe it.

Mitsu nodded.

Kat's fear turned to anger. That was *her* train and *her* town Dyscordia was trying to destroy. "Why? Why would she do that?"

Mitsu said, "She has taken all the energy that she can from our world. The few of us who did not fall prey to her protect what is left, but the damage has been done. To stay strong and survive, she had to go up."

Would Totsville share the same fate as Tutkium? A place with no Thanksgiving, where everyone hated each other? No! She had to do something.

"We have to stop her!" Kat screamed.

"I'm so happy to hear you say it, Kat McGee!" Mitsu said, relieved. "There is a way."

Kat looked at the map, which sat on the console in front of them. The words she didn't understand, the stars pulsing . . . Mitsu's explanations were starting to make sense.

"Gram told me there is always a way to help," Kat said. "I think I'm getting this. The map is showing us where we have to go to find the talisman, and the talisman is the key to running the Ten-Forty in Totsville. And if the Ten-Forty can run, and we can gather the food for the feast, the fighting in Totsville will stop. We'll have our Thanksgiving, and Dyscordia will lose!"

Mitsu nodded. "To defeat her, we must create something peaceful and happy again. To do that, we need the Talisman."

Kat got it, but she had another question for the ever-smiling Mitsu. She looked at him and asked, "But why would you help me and Totsville? You said the damage was already done to the Tunnels of Tutkium. right?"

"We help each other, Kat McGee! Dyscordia destroyed your train, and then took it a step further. She ensured that it would only run with the Tutkium Talisman, which she stole from our land." Mitsu looked at Kat.

"The Talisman was the symbol of respect, harmony, and tolerance here in Tutkium," he continued. "She took it, and then those qualities began to disappear from our people. Her evil ways give the negative new life. But since Dyscordia can only rule in a world of fear and anger and conflict, I believe that if we reverse the chaos she's inflicted, Dyscordia will disappear. We may be able to restore our happiness. The Tunnels of Tutkium may be saved."

The sparkle flittered into Mitsu's eyes again at the thought. "And maybe, just maybe," he added, "we could bring Potlatch back to Tutkium."

"Potlatch? What's that? Like a potluck?" Kat asked.

Mitsu laughed. "Tutkium's Potlatch," he said, "is like your Thanksgiving. All the kingdoms of Tutkium came together to celebrate Potlatch. It was a grand celebration of the harvest of each land, and it was very sacred."

Kat shook her head. "But you don't need me! I don't know anything about this world," she said, pointing at the map. "I don't know any magic. How would I know how to find the talisman? It's just like the Gobbler Games." Her heart dropped at the thought. "My brothers and sisters are right—I don't have a lot to offer."

"Nonsense!" Mitsu pointed at the words and the pulsing dots on the map.

"THE KEY TO THANKSGIVING GETS YOUR TRAIN BACK ON TRACK."

"The map is taking us to the worlds of Tutkium that have suffered most," Mitsu said. "We must go to them. I do not think we will find the Talisman, but we will find clues. If we seek the things the Talisman represents, perhaps the clues will get us to it."

"So we look for peace and harmony in all the places where everyone is angry and hates each other?" Kat thought that seemed like a daunting task. "I'm no peacemaker. I can't even get along with my brothers and sisters!"

Mitsu shook his head. "You do not give yourself enough credit, Kat McGee! You have to believe in yourself as a person who embodies and spreads the qualities of respect and peace.

And then you will. It may be the only way to save your world and mine!"

Kat thought about what Mitsu had told her. Pookcheensquas, Dyscordia, the Tunnels of Tutkium, magic, energy, chaos. . . it made her head spin! But she knew one thing for certain: If she didn't find the key—the Tutkium Talisman—fix the Ten-Forty, and return to Totsville in time, there would be no Thanksgiving.

And a Totsville without Thanksgiving was a Totsville Kat did not want to see.

"Do you believe, Kat McGee?" Mitsu begged.

Kat could see how much Mitsu wanted her help. She wasn't sure what she would do on the journey, and she certainly didn't know anything about trolls or chaos or maps or keys.

But Gram was right. This was her way to help. She knew what she had to do.

"If defeating Dyscordia means saving Thanksgiving," Kat gulped, "count me in."

Mitsu jumped out of his seat and grabbed Kat in a huge bear hug. "*Woliwon!* Kat McGee, *woliwon!*"

"Wully-what?" Kat asked. With her face smushed against Mitsu's sweater-like poncho, her voice was muffled. She doubted he'd heard her.

"*Woliwon* means thank you! Thank you, Kat McGee." Mitsu released her from the hug and held her at arm's distance, smiling the way Kat's mom did when she bought Kat a new dress. "Oh, let me look at you—you're so grown up!" Mrs. McGee would say. Kat always blushed and rolled her eyes because it made her feel like a little kid.

But Mitsu's smile conveyed something completely different. He was genuinely thankful to have Kat by his side. He truly believed she could help him. And she was on a flying train moving through tunnels far beneath the world she knew, trying to defeat an evil Pookcheen-something.

Before Kat could say "*woliwon*" back to Mitsu to thank him for being with her on this grand adventure, a dot on Gram's map began to flash and blink. Ahead, Kat could see the tunnel opening up, but nothing beyond that was visible. And still the Ten-Forty was racing toward the end of the tunnel.

"Buckle your belt, Kat McGee! This adventure is about to freefall!" Mitsu yelled as the train gained speed.

The tunnel opened up into a gargantuan cavern—and the train started to fall.

Fast.

"Ahhhhhooooooeeeee!" Kat screamed. She couldn't help herself. Goosebumps sprouted on her arms as she braced for impact. Was she scared? Yes. Was she nervous? Affirmative. But was she excited? Absolutely.

Kat did not feel like a little kid anymore.

CHAPTER 7
THE TROLLS OF INTOLERANCE

A low growl came from the cave as Malsom and his mistress stepped out into the darkness of a deep forest of jagged rocks.

"The trolls will take care of them. I am sure of it," Dyscordia said to the wolf. "But if they somehow escape alive, that will put them one step closer to us and the Talisman. We must take care of them before they go any further. Do you understand, my pet?"

The wolf howled softly.

"Excellent," Dyscordia snarled. "In the meantime, we'll let the trolls have their fun."

She smiled maliciously into the damp, heavy air.

Without opening her eyes, Kat felt her arms, legs, and face. *OK,* she decided. *I think I'm still alive.*

Kat opened one eye. She saw Mitsu beside her, his huge smile still stretched across his face, like they had just gone for a leisurely stroll in the park. She opened the other eye—the Ten-Forty seemed to have held together. Still disheveled and thrashed, but in one piece nonetheless.

"But . . . we were going so fast," Kat said, baffled. "I thought for sure we were going to crash!"

"Trolltropolis is much deeper down in the Tunnels of Tutkium," Mitsu explained.

"How far below the ground are we?" Kat asked.

"Well, let me say this. It would be too far for you to dig with your gardening tools," Mitsu laughed. "I think in terms of your miles, it is 3958.8 from the Earth's surface to its center. Our world is somewhere in the middle," Mitsu explained.

Wow. That's a lot farther than any training run for the Gobbler Games, Kat thought.

Mitsu unbuckled his seatbelt, stood, and stretched, yawning as if he'd just awoken from a long, comfortable nap. Kat felt more like she'd just stumbled off the scariest, strangest ride at Magic Isles in Thrillville.

"They will know we are coming, so we must have a plan ready. They may not kill us, but they won't like us being here, either," Mitsu said nonchalantly.

Kat gasped. If Mitsu was trying to make her feel better, he was failing miserably. "W-w-what's our plan?"

Seeing Kat's nervousness, Mitsu tried to calm her. "Do not worry! We have an ally in Trolltropolis! Wanagamesuk will help us! He is expecting us!"

Kat looked out the window. For the first time, she did not see a tunnel. The Ten-Forty's cab had landed in a ghostly dark world.

A black river ran through the forested land. Huge, moss-covered boulders surrounding short, dead tree trunks flanked each side of the flowing water. Everything was a colorless dark gray, muddy brown, midnight blue, or black as night—each plant, rock, or small tree looked slimier and dirtier than the last. Long globs of moss hung from charcoal branches. In the darkness that surrounded them, Kat could not see how far the cave world extended. They were in a marsh, quite a distance from the nearest rock formations.

They stepped off the train and into the dark, wet surroundings. The blackness was disconcerting. Unfortunately, Hannah hadn't been completely wrong when she accused Kat of being afraid of the dark. Kat wouldn't necessarily say she was afraid—but given the choice she did prefer a night-light. Now she was in creepy Trolltropolis hundreds of miles under the ground, trying to not freak out.

Kat's teeth began to chatter. This sometimes happened when she was nervous. And cold.

Then, to her horror, Kat's feet began to sink into the mud. Hearing her startled gasp, Mitsu closed his eyes and reached down to touch her feet.

"*Nsit chigonak*," he mumbled. "*Nsit chigonak*."

A hard, tortoise-like shell appeared, covering Kat's shoes and extending up her calves like rain boots.

Next Mitsu put his hands over Kat's ears, making them feel warm. Her teeth stopped chattering and she experienced a sense of calm washing over her.

Mitsu smiled, happy with the results. "Now you can walk without fear of sinking or getting muddy walking shoes! And no chattering of teeth!"

Kat looked at Mitsu, then at her feet, amazed. She touched her ears and face—wow! She already felt better. Her eyes were adjusting to the darkness, and she could see the shadows of rocks and trees.

Jumping up and down in her surprisingly comfortable shell shoes, Kat asked, "How did you do that?!"

"That is what I do! I help people. Now *espons*, we wait for Wanagamesuk. We will only be safe with him!"

So they waited. And waited.

"Are you sure Wanagamesuk is coming?" Kat asked. "Will he know how to find the key?"

Out of the darkness came a noise.

"Wisssssuh."

Mitsu responded, "Wissssuh-me-oh."

A creature unlike any Kat had ever seen emerged from the shadows. His face was so thin that it was hard to see him unless he turned his head. His eyes were narrow black slits the width of a dime; his mouth was a hollow hole that never opened or closed. Hundreds of rocks formed his narrow arms, legs, and torso, as if they were somehow glued together in the shape of a body.

Kat had seen the *Lord of the Rings* trilogy (and loved it), and this creature was nothing like those trolls. Trolls were supposed to be big and hairy and belch a lot. Like how her sister Emily always called Abe a troll when he burped at the dinner table.

This . . . thing was completely different.

Mitsu walked a few steps to meet Wanagamesuk, and the two of them mumbled words that Kat couldn't understand. Together they returned to Kat.

Kristin Riddick

The rock troll spoke first. A voice emerged from the hollow crevice in his face, which still did not move. "Welcome, young *espons*. I am sorry you came all this way to complete a most impossible task."

Kat looked at Mitsu. She had been so overwhelmed with information and the prospect of saving Thanksgiving that they hadn't discussed the details of making peace between these enemies or finding clues to the whereabouts of the Talisman.

Their treasure hunt was leading nowhere fast.

"It is only a slight problem," Mitsu explained. "If there is a clue here to finding the Talisman, then there is only one way to proceed. And that is to go to the head of Trolltropolis, Kugu. Unfortunately, Dyscordia and Kugu are what your people call BFFs."

Kat couldn't suppress a giggle.

Mitsu continued. "If Kugu doesn't know where the Talisman is, she'll know how to find it. But it is impossible to see her without going through the rock trolls first. They will do anything Kugu says, but they despise humans. They will cut off our fingers before we have a chance to say *tan khak*."

Kat gulped. "Umm, that sounds horrible. But we can't turn back. We have to go and show her how important this is. How important Potlatch is."

Wanagamesuk looked at the small child. "You were right, Mitsu. Much courage in this one."

Mitsu nodded. "It is risky, but we will need to pretend we have been captured. Wanagamesuk can get us to Kugu. But I don't know what she will do to us."

Double gulp.

"You will have only one chance," Wanagamesuk said. "If you can convince Kugu to tell you where the Talisman is hidden, that will mean she trusts and respects you. And that may be enough to break Dyscordia's spell over the other trolls. They have been enveloped by her negative energy and hatred for too long. Perhaps you can free them."

"Me?!" Kat asked. "How am I supposed to do that?"

Mitsu looked down at his feet. "I told you I would need many things from you, Kat McGee. Here is the first. Dyscordia's spell over the rock trolls was born of their fighting, remember? We must show her a better way. The rock trolls inhabited Tutkium even before the Malimaquiddies. They were always welcoming to my people. Kugu must remember why we are friends and not enemies."

"But I hate talking to adults," Kat whined. "When I talk to teachers, I'm a bumbling mess. How am I going to talk to a rock troll queen?"

Mitsu's eyes glistened. "We can go back."

It was tempting, but Kat knew she had no choice. They had to find the talisman, and if Kugu knew where it was, then they had to go to Kugu.

Mitsu and Wanagamesuk looked at each other, waiting for her answer.

After a long pause, Kat asked, "Which way to the rock troll queen?"

Without another word, they were on their way.

The family training for the Gobbler Games had helped Kat prepare for the journey to the heart of Trolltropolis. The trio climbed up rocks, cut through rocks, slid around rocks, and crossed the black river twice.

Kat spent the journey listening to her new friends. They were kind enough to speak English so that she could understand, though Kat did hear a few mumbles, whispers, and words from their own languages that made her want to learn more than just *tan khak* and *espons*.

They talked of the time before Dyscordia, when the rock trolls and humans were friendly. They spoke of Potlatch, of celebrating in their separate tunnel worlds and then together, of bountiful harvests, good trading, and learning about each other's land.

Dyscordia—though they often called her Pookcheensquas—put a stop to all of that. The trolls and Malimaquiddies were now bitter enemies.

"But why do *you* not hate Mitsu and his people?" Kat asked.

Wanagamesuk turned to Kat. "I do not believe in hurting other people because they are different from me. I have deep respect for Mitsu, just as he does for me. That he looks and speaks and eats in ways I think strange makes no difference. *Espons*, I am immune to Dyscordia's spells and dark magic because I have a strong mind and an open heart. I have found a few like me in our midst, but Dyscordia poisons those who fear others and are afraid of change."

Kat thought about this. At the Thanksgiving Feast in Totsville, many families had different skin colors, spoke other languages, and brought interesting types of foods. But Kat didn't see why those differences were bad. Her mom had told her that on the inside, the other families were just like the McGees. They might not know the same games, or dress the same way, but Kat had learned there was no reason to be scared of those differences.

So why would the trolls and humans be scared of each other?

Their story sounded familiar, but Kat couldn't put her finger on why.

And before she could figure it out, she fell flat on her face.

The young adventurer picked herself up, blushing. She was glad it was so dark that Mitsu and Wanagamesuk couldn't see her red cheeks.

In the next instant, though, Kat forgot her embarrassment. She looked up, and before her was the grand set of stone steps that would lead them to Kugu's chamber.

Wanagamesuk raised his rocky arms. "I will tie your hands so that you will look like my prisoners. All are prepared to fight to capture you, but I will say I snuck out so I could find you first."

Kat looked at Mitsu, who nodded. She swallowed hard, hoping she could gulp her fear away. They put their hands behind their backs and allowed them to be secured with a slimy, slick moss that was strong as rope. Kat felt like a character in one of Gus's weird video games.

"We won't have much time before you are thrown in the Hole of Hurt. You will need to act fast," Wanagamesuk said, his voice serious.

Hole of Hurt? Kat didn't want to know why it had that name.

The two fake prisoners followed Wanagamesuk up the broad stairs. As they climbed, they heard chanting, yelling, and arguing from inside the rocky cave.

At the top, they walked into the midst of a mob of rock trolls who looked almost identical to Wanagamesuk. Some were taller or shorter, darker shades of rock or lighter. Some had rock arms and legs that were longer or shorter. But all of them held spears or blunt hammers. Their rock faces expressed nothing, but to Kat, their voices sounded angry.

Kugu, ruler of the rock trolls, sat on a towering river rock at the end of the room. A crown of moss was perched atop her head. Next to her was a massive hole in the stone floor.

The Hole of Hurt.

Great, Kat thought.

Kat nudged Mitsu, but he would not look up. "Keep your gaze down, Kat McGee!" He whispered. Still, it sounded like an exclamation.

Kugu stared down at them. Then a booming, scratchy voice emerged from her hollowed-out stone mouth. "What a surprise! Wanagamesuk has brought us dinner?" She asked it as a question but Kat hoped no one would answer.

Kat heard a clicking. When she looked down, she saw that the shells of her new boots were hitting each other. She was literally shaking in her boots! Kat was so scared that she knew her teeth would start chattering soon too.

Wanagamesuk bowed. "You asked, so I delivered."

The trolls erupted in shouts of anger—anger at Kat, and at each other. All around her, Kat felt tension and anger and fear in the air.

The swarm of the rock creatures parted as Wanagamesuk pushed his prisoners to the front of the room. They stood below Kugu's throne—just a few steps away from the Hole of Hurt.

The rock troll queen rose, quieting the crowd.

"You have returned," Kugu said to Mitsu. "I thought we were very clear. You are no longer welcome in our land."

Mitsu lifted his chin and looked steadily at Kugu. "I believe it is time to reconcile."

"There will be no reconciliation with savages who steal from us!" Kugu bellowed. "And you!" she screamed, pointing at Kat. "How dare you enter my domain! Have you come to see our Hole of Hurt?"

The rock trolls laughed and cheered.

Kat was too scared to respond, so Mitsu spoke. "You know we mean the rock trolls no harm. This war is not what we wanted. Dyscordia has misled you."

Kugu lifted her spear and pointed it at Mitsu. "You dare to insult Pookcheensquas?"

"Look at me. I am your friend." A gentle smile appeared on Mitsu's face. "Don't you remember?"

Kat was shocked. How could Mitsu be so calm and respectful when this creature was trying to throw them into a pit of pain? She wanted to grab a rock or a spear, do something to hurt these horrible trolls and escape!

But then Kat realized why Mitsu's stories had sounded so familiar.

Thanksgiving.

In school, Kat had learned about the very first Thanksgiving celebration. The differences between the Pilgrims and the Native Americans were much like those between Mitsu's people and the rock trolls. Mitsu was trying to do what the Native Americans in Plymouth had done.

He was showing respect to Kugu, in the hopes of saving all of them, even when being respectful was the hardest thing to do.

But Kugu was having none of it. How was Kat supposed to convince her that Dyscordia was wrong? How could she make Kugu see them as friends, not enemies? If she even knew something about the Tutkium Talisman, would she ever tell them?

Kugu knocked her spear on the floor three times.

On the second pounding, the chant began: "Hole. Of. Hurt . . . Hole. Of. Hurt."

The surrounding rocks shook. The ground trembled beneath the trolls' pounding weapons.

"Take the old man first. The Hole of Hurt will teach him the difference between friends and enemies," Kugu demanded.

Kat panicked. They couldn't throw Mitsu in there! He had done so much for her already! Without him, she'd be all alone, which surely spelled doom.

Two rock trolls grabbed Mitsu and led him toward the hole.

Kat didn't have time to think. She had to do something. She had to show Kugu that she and Mitsu were worth saving.

"Stop!" Kat yelled.

But even Kat's most vehement shout was swallowed up in the din of the trolls.

Kat leaped up and ran beside Mitsu, trying to throw her body in front of his.

"Throw me first!" she cried. "This is your world, and we came here unannounced and uninvited. But you used to welcome people like us. Mitsu respects you, and I respect Mitsu. If this is your decision, we have to accept it. I am the reason Mitsu came here. So you must throw me into Hole of Hurt first."

The rock trolls gasped.

Kat couldn't believe her own words, but she had made up her mind. She turned toward the hole, closed her eyes, and thought of how scared those first Pilgrims and Native Americans must have been of each other. It would have taken a huge leap of faith for them to trust the strange beings that didn't speak their language, who dressed and ate and talked differently.

Kat was going to do the same.

The jeers stopped; the room was silent. Mitsu, Wanagamesuk, Kugu, and every troll in the vast chamber stared at Kat.

Kat opened her eyes and looked down. *Yikes.*

The Hole of Hurt was aptly named. Pointed bones jutted so far out of the walls that their sharpened points almost touched. Kat couldn't see the bottom of the hole, but red eyes and white teeth glared at her from a drop of at least 20 feet. And whatever was down there was growling.

"Kat McGee!" Mitsu whispered. "Don't do this."

Without hesitating another moment, Kat took a step closer.

A crowd of trolls moved to surround the hole, intently watching Kat.

She lifted her foot, trying to imagine jumping into the water at Lake Cimarron instead of a den of beady-eyed monsters. As she was about to leap she heard a grunt behind her.

"WAIT!"

Kugu had stepped off her throne and come toward Kat. Something was different. Her voice had changed.

The sound that emanated from her unmoving rock mouth was no longer a bellowed scream.

"You would jump into the Hole of Hurt for this old man? You would do as I say and risk death? I have never seen such things from a human, much less a human child."

Kat remembered what Mitsu said had been stolen by Dyscordia: respect, peace, and harmony. She looked at Kugu and said, "Mitsu has told me of the respect and tolerance you used to have for each other. I am only trying to show the same to you and to him, since I am the reason we are here."

"And what is that reason?" Kugu asked.

Kat swallowed. "To find the Tutkium Talisman. It is the key my train needs to run so that I may go home. It is the only way we can have Thanksgiving."

Kugu looked at Mitsu. "Is this Thanksgiving like our Potlatch?"

Mitsu nodded.

Again, the cave went silent.

Kugu was torn. She had never received such respect or seen such courage from a little human. Her anger and fear began to falter.

"Why should I save you, little girl?" she demanded.

If I were in Kugu's shoes, why would I want to help? Kat asked herself. She thought of Totsville, the Ten-Forty, and the Thanksgiving Feast.

"If we find the Talisman," she said, her voice shaking slightly, "it will bring happiness to a lot of people. Not just in Tutkium, but in my world too."

The cave was still.

Kugu took two steps toward Kat. The rock troll queen wasn't much taller than she was. A gold ring on a string of moss hung from her rock neck. Kat had not noticed it before. Though Kugu's rock face still showed no expression, she reached and took the string of moss and hung it around Kat's neck.

"I don't know where to find the Talisman, but I believe this will help," Kugu said.

The string of moss was slimy, but the ring was warm, even through her hoodie, much like Mitsu's hands. Kat looked down at the ring and saw it was a key ring.

She didn't know what it would do, if anything, but she was so thankful. Impulsively, she reached out and gave Kugu a hug.

The cave of rock trolls erupted in applause. Again, they pounded their weapons and began to chant, but this chant was different.

"Kat Mc-Gee. Find the key. Kat Mc-Gee. Find the key."

Kugu motioned for the rock trolls to release Mitsu. Then she pounded her spear and the cave quieted once again. "Take care of this one, Mitsu. She is special. I am worried for your journey, but I hope you will find the Talisman. Pookcheensquas will try to punish us all, but we will be ready."

Mitsu's smile returned. "We will be ready together. You know the Malimaquiddies will stand by your side."

"I have been in a fog of hate and anger," Kugu said, "but it is lifting now, and I remember how things should be. We will respect your people as you have respected us."

Kat smiled as the old friends joined hand to rock. She looked down once more before they left at the bones jutting out into the darkness.

Adios, Hole of Hurt. Kat thought. *One down, two to go.*

CHAPTER 8

CLOSE ENCOUNTERS OF THE DYSCORDIA KIND

Dyscordia fell back, staggering as if she'd been hit in the gut. Slowly, she regained her balance, but she could still feel the rush of pain through her body. With a slight shiver, she looked at her nails. The steel talons were three inches shorter.

"Nooooo!" she shouted, the echo of the cave drowning out her screams.

"I should have known better than to trust those miserable rock trolls!" She spat, enraged. "How could Kugu have let this happen?"

The Pookcheensquas snapped her fingers and the scene in the cave pool disappeared. She looked into the dark water, now black as stone. One brown eye and one green eye stared back at her rather than the midnight blue glow she had grown accustomed to seeing.

"Malsom, we must take care of them now," she snarled.

That foolish girl would not get her dirty little hands on the key. She and her trusted wolf would see to that.

"I'm not afraid of the Hole of Hurt. I'm not afraid of the Hole of Hurt. I'm—"

Kat jerked her head up and opened her eyes. She was talking in her sleep again.

Beside her, Mitsu was steering what was left of the Ten-Forty. Kat looked ahead. The Ten-Forty's light pointed into the darkness of the tunnel before them.

So the dream was real?! Kat wondered. *I'm in the Tunnels of Tutkium and we just survived the rock trolls of Trolltropolis?* She felt blindly for the ring around her neck. *Wow. Kugu really did help us.*

But how? How did the key ring get them closer to the key? What did this have to do with the Talisman? And what was the next clue?

That's when Kat's eyes were pulled to the map.

"THE KEY TO THANKSGIVING GETS YOUR TRAIN BACK ON TRACK. THREE IS THE MAGIC NUMBER TO FIND YOUR WAY BACK."

And beneath those words, two new statements had appeared.

"THE TALISMAN'S RING IS A PIECE YOU WILL NEED. FIND THE HORN OF PLENTY TO HELP PLANT YOUR NEXT SEED."

Mitsu looked at the next blinking light on Gram's map and nodded his head vigorously. "See Kat McGee? The map knows we have the key ring, so it is showing us where to go next! And this will be nothing like Trolltropolis, I can assure you!"

"What's a horn of plenty?" Kat asked. "Something good?"

Mitsu's eyes twinkled. "Do you know what a cornucopia is?"

Kat smiled. She finally knew something! "Yes! My mom puts one in the center of our dining room table for the whole month of November. It's shaped like a horn!"

"Yes, Kat McGee! Cornucopia means 'horn of plenty,' and in Greek mythology it was fabled to be the horn of the goat nymph Amalthaea, whose milk was fed to the baby Zeus! Just like in your world, it has long been a symbol of fruitfulness and abundance here in Tutkium. I'm pleasantly surprised the map is telling us to go there."

Kat's sister Hannah loved the Greek gods and goddesses. She couldn't wait to tell her where the word cornucopia originated.

"Cornucopia is a land in Tutkium?" Kat asked. She didn't remember seeing it on the map.

"Oh yes! It is a most merry place indeed," Mitsu said with a chuckle. "I was hoping the map would take us to Cornucopia, because it is the only place in Tutkium that has remained immune to Dyscordia's spells. It is where we all used to gather for Potlatch. You will soon see why."

Mitsu pressed a button, and they shot forward like a turbo train.

"Hold on to your hats! Cornucopia here we come!" Mitsu exclaimed.

All right! If Dyscordia wasn't in Cornucopia, then Kat was ready.

Then she remembered what her mom always told her:

Be careful what you ask for.

The Ten-Forty slowly ascended a tunnel, crawling upward like a rollercoaster ready to plunge to the ground. Kat wondered how far they'd traveled from Trolltropolis. It seemed like they'd been flying through the Tunnels of Tutklum forever!

"You said Cornucopia was merry?" Kat asked. She'd only heard that word used to describe Christmas. "Why is it merry?"

Before Mitsu could answer, the train stopped climbing. He pushed a few buttons, but they still didn't move. The lights on the control panel started to spark and falter. The headlight dimmed and flashed, as if the power was about to go out completely.

Something was wrong.

As if on cue, the mysterious train voice shouted a warning, "Danger ahead. Please secure your belts. Danger ahead."

And then, a shadow stepped into the headlight.

"Going somewhere?" a voice boomed.

Kat looked up. Standing in front of the train was a being scarier than any rock troll. The tall woman's hair swirled like a mass of snakes slithering on her head. Fury lit her face. And her fingers were pointed directly at them, the steel talons sparking at the tips as though lightning bolts might be released at any moment.

Dyscordia.

"Get them!" the woman screamed.

Before Kat and Mitsu knew what was happening, an angry black wolf lunged from the shadows and leaped on top of the train, clawing ferociously at the windshield. Instinctively Kat ducked, hiding as much of her body as she could. The thin pane of glass that separated her from the angry wolf didn't seem like nearly enough protection.

With a hiss, Dyscordia shoved her outstretched fingers toward the window next to Mitsu. Blue lightning bolts shot from her steel fingertips. The window shattered. The huge wolf jumped to the side of the car and tried to lunge through the window at Mitsu. Mitsu ducked, barely escaping his claws.

"What do we do?" Kat shouted.

"We must hug," Mitsu cried, crawling to Kat's side of the conductor's cab.

"Wh-what?" Alarmed, Kat looked out the window behind Mitsu. Malsom, all teeth and drool, was about to jump through the broken glass pane and devour them. How in the world was a *hug* going to help?

Kat covered her eyes. *I'm doomed!*

Undaunted, Mitsu threw his arms around Kat and shouted, "Kat McGee, you are such a wonderful friend! I am having so much fun! I hope you will stay in Tutkium for many moons!"

The lightning bolts faded. Dyscordia faltered, taking a dizzying step back.

With a nod of his head, Mitsu urged Kat to follow his lead. She hugged him back harder and shouted, "Mitsu, you are the greatest guide a girl could ever ask for! You saved my life, and you're helping me find my way home. Thank you for being my friend!"

Dyscordia's face was twisted in rage, but the Pookcheensquas was powerless against the stream of kind words. She tried to cover her ears and close her eyes, not wanting to hear or see them. Malsom fell off the train with a thump, as if an invisible force had thrown him.

Mitsu kept hugging Kat, trying to smile and say the most positive things he could think of. "Your Gram is the sweetest woman I know!"

At the mention of Gram, Kat briefly forgot her fear. "How I love Gram and her turkey tamales!"

Dyscordia tried to thrust her nails of steel toward Kat and Mitsu again, but now the bolts of lightning that had exploded from her fingertips with such force disintegrated before hitting them.

Stunned, Kat looked at a weakened Dyscordia in front of the train. She fell back farther into the tunnel. Her steel fingers had shrunk another inch.

Malsom, panting, ran to his mistress's side.

"I . . . must get . . . out of here," Dyscordia huffed.

She threw her cape around the wolf, and in the blink of an eye, they disappeared.

CHAPTER 9
THE MERRY MAIDS OF CORNUCOPIA

Mitsu climbed back over to the conductor's chair and put his hands in the space where the window had been. He chanted softly, and the broken pieces of glass slowly melded back together, linking up like puzzle pieces until a solid window appeared.

Kat shook her head. "Umm . . . hello? Couldn't you have used some of that magic to make Dyscordia disappear? That wolf was a little too close for comfort. I could smell his grody dog breath!"

Mitsu laughed. "I am not what you call a superhero, Kat McGee—I am more of a healer! Dyscordia is too powerful. And what we did was not magic at all! Like I told you, Dyscordia can only survive in chaos. If there is love and peace, she is weakened. I'm sure she is now trying to regain her strength by hiding in some of the chaos she's created."

"Will she be back?" Kat asked timidly.

Mitsu sighed, "I'm afraid so. Or we will have to find her. She is the only one who knows where to find the Talisman."

The lights of the Ten-Forty brightened, and the train finally started climbing again. Before Kat could protest the idea of meeting Dyscordia for a second time, the Ten-Forty took a nosedive off the lip of a tunnel and plummeted down into what looked like an ocean of water.

WHOOSH! Kat braced herself. Water was everywhere, yet not a drop leaked into the cab of the busted up Ten-Forty.

Mitsu's magic is definitely helping us out here, Kat thought.

All around, she saw myriad sea creatures and plants, seaweed-covered rocks and stunning coral reefs. *The Ten-Forty's like a submarine!* Kat thought in wonder. *With a little help, this relic can do anything!*

The train splashed and floated up, down, and all around, until it finally landed on solid ground. The voice announced, "Welcome to Cornucopia. Home of the merry Marys," and Mitsu stood up, a big smile on his face.

"Why, thank you, SJ!" he called.

"Who is SJ?" Kat said, stopping him. "Where are you going? You can't get out here! Aren't we under water?"

Mitsu laughed. "Oh no, Kat McGee. We are not on the ocean floor. The ocean is above us! We have landed beneath the water."

Kat was incredulous. "There's a land beneath the ocean?"

"Hurry up and you will see!" Mitsu said, already halfway out the door.

When Kat stepped off the train, her jaw dropped. Mitsu was right! Instead of clouds or sky, tunnels or caves or dirt, all she saw above her was water. Sure enough, the ocean the Ten-Forty had plunged through was now above them.

"A sky of water. That's maybe the coolest thing I've ever seen!" she said, dazzled.

When Kat brought her eyes down, she gulped. Twenty tall, curvy women with pink faces, indigo hands, white horns on their heads, and very long necks stood before them.

"Omigarsh!" Kat exclaimed. "The women! I've seen them! When Gram gave me the map!"

"That's the magic of the map," Mitsu said. "A young lady holding it can see part of the journey that awaits her." He gestured toward the women, as if tipping an invisible hat on his head. "Welcome to Cornucopia. Former home of the Potlatch Feast."

As he said the words, Mitsu seemed to be increasing his pace toward the gaggle of women.

Kat hurried to keep up and soon saw the reason for Mitsu's haste.

Every merry maid of Cornucopia held a different kind of miniature cake. Mitsu bowed to one, and she handed him a coconut cake.

Kat felt her stomach growl. She realized she was starving!

The closest woman smiled broadly, revealing glistening, golden teeth. "Oh, Kat McGee! What a pleasure to see! We're so happy to finally meet thee!"

She turned to another merry maid, who held a tiny carrot cake. "Do you see, Mary? How excited are we? We're finally meeting Kat McGee!"

Two other women grabbed Kat's arms and guided her through the crowd. "Come have a seat!" one chirped. "You must want to eat. And we have many, many, many a treat."

"But she may want to rest," the woman on Kat's other arm said. "We must do our best. You know they're on a very important quest."

"I know, dear Mary," the other replied. "I'm not being contrary, but first to tea—we mustn't tarry!"

"Are they all named Mary?" Kat whispered to Mitsu.

He didn't need to answer. In unison, everyone around Kat stopped and said, "We are, yessiree! It's easy to see. If you please, call us all Mary!"

As they led Kat and Mitsu down a rainbow path, Kat looked at them closely. Each merry maid had a round pink face, indigo hands, a white horn on her head, and golden teeth. While they all wore plain white dresses, each one had small, unique qualities, too. One had a star on her cheek. Another wore striped knee socks. One had a ribbon on her head. Every Mary was different.

Kat whispered to Mitsu, "They all look alike except for one thing!"

"Well, of course they do! They're sisters!" Mitsu said.

The family of Marys led Kat and Mitsu around their village, which was brighter and happier than any cartoon Kat had ever seen on television. How was this all underground, beneath a humongous body of water? It seemed completely unreal!

The huts were the colors of the rainbow, and gardens of bright vegetables grew around each one. Singing birds perched on the Marys' shoulders, and waterfalls poured down from certain parts of the ocean sky. Flowers of every color and variety bloomed, brightening the village even more.

Mitsu broke into a broad smile at Kat's amazement.

"You should have seen it during Potlatch! Imagine people like us, the rock trolls, and the merry maids—a celebration of mythical proportions! You know, the Greeks and Romans celebrated the harvest too! Cornucopia!!"

"That's right!" Kat remembered Hannah dressing up like the Greek goddess Demeter for Halloween. She'd claimed she deserved more candy because she was the Goddess of the Harvest. Hannah would love Cornucopia—it was mythical indeed!

The merry maids gave Kat a waterfall ocean shower while washing her clothes. Mitsu and Kat ate a delicious meal that ended with fourteen bites of different flavors of cake. Kat watched in awe, and Mitsu was in hog heaven.

"Almost as good as my turkey tamales," Mitsu mumbled.

"*Your* turkey tamales?!" Kat had been meaning to ask Mitsu about that ever since he mentioned Gram during their horrible Dyscordia encounter. She'd thought Gram's Turkey Day Tamales were one-of-a-kind!

Mitsu smiled. "Oh yes! Before Dyscordia, my turkey tamales were the hit of Potlatch! Your gram loved them! Yes, Cornucopia brought us all together. The merry Marys know all there is to know about our world, and they celebrated every part of it. Their joy was contagious and brought us all together. They knew you were in Tutkium the moment you landed."

The merry Marys entranced Kat. They were in constant motion—they never stopped working, moving, or talking! Some cooked, some cleaned; some fed the many animals in the village. Others gathered food or drove small chariots, while some fixed fences or worked in the shop. Some were painting, and others were building. Every Mary had something to do—kind of like the chores all the McGee kids got while preparing for Thanksgiving.

"Why haven't Dyscordia's evil tricks affected the merry maids?" Kat asked.

"Well, the reason her powers don't work here are the same reason it may be difficult to find our next clue," Mitsu explained. "You see, Kat McGee, the merry maids can *only* be merry. They know no other emotions. They only see good in people, and so they can't be sad or mad. They can only be glad." Mitsu smiled at his own Cornucopia rhyme.

Kat's eyes widened. She hated being upset or angry. "Awesome! How lucky are they?"

Mitsu shook his head. "You don't understand, *espons*. They aren't capable of changing—not at all. They don't grow old or understand time. Dyscordia cannot change their mind, and she uses this to her advantage. Of course she can't step foot in Cornucopia—their joy would destroy her. But she sends her minions to deceive them, and they do not know the difference."

"Oh, that's terrible! And cruel," Kat said. "Then how will we find the clue to the Talisman? How will we know where to go next?"

"I'm not sure," Mitsu said. "But there's only one way to find out!"

"What's that?"

His dimples deepened. "We ask! But we must ask correctly."

Kat wrinkled her nose, confused. "Like, say 'please'?"

"No, no," Mitsu said, smiling. "Kat McGee, you must ask in a way they understand: in rhyme!"

Kat thought for a minute. She loved rhymes but wasn't sure if she could make them up right on the spot. She tapped the nearest Mary's shoulder. "Do you know where the Tutkium Talisman may be? Because we really need to find that key!"

A huge smile spread across her face. She thought of a rhyme under pressure! Her mom would be so proud.

The Mary smiled back, nodded, and grabbed a nearby Mary. "Oh Mary, our guests want to know! A clue for the key, where do they go?"

A merry Mary wearing blue gloves shuffled over to them. "Follow me. I'll show you what I can. We'd love to help with your plan. Maybe then you'll more often visit our clan!"

Kat smiled. She would love to come back here. She wanted to come back with Gram—or Hannah. They would have so much fun with the merry maids of Cornucopia.

The blue-gloved maid led Mitsu and Kat to a chariot. No horse was attached to the front. *How will it move?* Kat thought.

"To the barn we must go! Don't be like a turtle and slow. We may have a clue to show!"

As soon as the rhyme was out of the Mary's mouth, the chariot began to move, speeding down the rainbow road toward a barn the size of Maine. The thing was huge!

Kat shouldn't have been surprised. An invisibly led chariot was certainly not the weirdest thing she'd seen in the last couple of days.

The merry maid stood at the door of the massive barn and said, "Here it is—if it's a key you seek. Many are here, some bright, some bleak. Let me know when you're done with your peek!"

The barn doors opened, as if on command.

Blue-gloved Mary smiled broadly, got in the chariot, whispered a rhyme, and rode off back to the village, her golden teeth sparkling.

Kat's jaw practically fell to the ground, and Mitsu laughed again. The Mary wasn't kidding. Keys were stacked, hung, and lined up from floor to ceiling. Tiny keys, big keys, wooden keys, rubber keys, paper keys, rainbow keys . . .

"I told you; they have a key to everything in Tutkium! Literally and . . ." Mitsu looked at Kat, eyebrows raised.

Kat caught her cue. "Figuratively! So now what do we do? How will we know if the Talisman is here? It would take years to go through all these keys."

"That," Mitsu said, "is the million-dollar question."

The glowing pool at the bottom of the cave showed the merry maids of Cornucopia dancing, laughing, and smiling as they pampered Kat and Mitsu.

"Cornucopia!" Dyscordia fumed. She swept her hand through the water, shattering the image. "I knew I should have done this myself!"

But even as she screamed, her voice quivered. She staggered back against the cave wall, her body shaking with weakness.

Dyscordia was furious with herself. She should have eliminated the girl once and for all in the tunnels. Now, she felt her body betraying her, losing energy with every movement. And all because of that little pestering child!

"If those smiling, happy nitwits point them to the key, I'll only have one more chance," she hissed. "But this time, I will not fail."

Dyscordia looked at her nails. The steel shrank before her eyes, only incensing her more.

"I will make them pay for what they are doing to me."

Kat was a little annoyed—and a lot tired. Searching for one particular magic key among thousands while the merry Marys had a grand ol' time in their amazing village was not her idea of fun.

"How do we know we're even looking for the Talisman?" She cried, exasperated. "I thought we were just looking for a *clue* that would help us *find* the talisman."

Mitsu sighed. "That's the problem, Kat McGee. We don't know."

"Well that's not fair," Kat whined. "It shouldn't be this hard! Can't the merry maids help us?"

After what Mitsu had told her, Kat didn't know how much help the merry Marys would be, but she couldn't help but complain. She and Mitsu were on a deadline, after all! And the Marys—well, they only . . . *rhymed—*

Wait a minute! Maybe that would work?!

The chariot. The barn door. Everything here had started moving . . . after a Mary said a rhyme.

Kat needed to think of another rhyme—a rhyme that would lead them to the Tutkium Talisman.

"Mitsu! Mitsu!" she yelled. He was somewhere on the other side of the barn.

Kat couldn't see him, but she heard his voice.

"What's going on? What do you need, Kat McGee?"

"A rhyme! Maybe we can find what we're looking for with a rhyme! Like the merry Marys!"

"Kat McGee! So smart! I will help you!" Mitsu crawled and fumbled over to Kat and smiled encouragingly. "Try first!"

"Talisman, talisman, if you are here . . . Please help us out and start to appear!"

Silence.

Mitsu tried. "If the key is not here for us to find, can you give us a clue? Oh, please be kind!"

Kat laughed. Rhyming was fun. But still no movement.

Mitsu smiled and closed his eyes. He put one hand over Kat's, and she closed hers, too. His hands were warm and calming.

"We should think of Thanksgiving. Of Potlatch. Of what it means for us to find the Talisman," Mitsu whispered.

Kat tried to think about the best parts of Thanksgiving—the things she would miss most if it were gone: Gram's Turkey Day tamales, the Mehtas' curried stuffing, and, of course, the Gobbler Games.

Then she whispered, "For the Gobbler Games and Potlatch and the Thanksgiving Feast, please point the way to the north, south, west, or east."

Mitsu squeezed Kat's shoulder. He finished the rhyme. "For friends and family to reunite and celebrate. We beg for a clue before it's too late!"

Kat and Mitsu opened their eyes. Kat wasn't sure what to expect, but the silence and stillness were not good signs.

"Why did I think this would work?" Kat stomped around in circles, hands waving in the air. "What a stupid idea! We didn't find anything!"

"Patience, *espons*. This world works in mysterious ways. Let us head back to the Ten-Forty."

Kat, head hung low, started shuffling her feet back toward the battered train.

That's when the light breeze suddenly turned to a strong wind. Mitsu looked up. The ocean above them had begun to darken, as if a huge whale had swum overhead and blocked out the sun.

Frightened, Kat grabbed Mitsu's arm. The wind was so strong that she was afraid she'd blow away. Rain droplets quickly became sheets of water, pouring over them. Then it started hailing! And snowing! On top of the rain!

"What's going on?" Kat shouted, her voice almost drowned out by the elements.

"Dyscordia," Mitsu said. "She's trying to get in. The happiness and harmony will kill her if she gets too close, but she will not stop trying to turn us against one another. She thinks a harsher environment may get the Marys fighting, but she is wrong. We should find shelter. This could get dangerous."

The dynamic duo barely made it back to the Ten-Forty before the deluge became too much to bear. Kat couldn't even say a proper good-bye to the merry Marys; she had to settle for a wave through the Ten-Forty's window. As Mitsu had predicted, the merry maids didn't seem to notice the rain, sleet, and snow pouring down on their village. They went about their business as if it was a bright and sunny day.

Kat was both happy and sad as she watched the merry Marys head back to their village under the ocean. Sad because they hadn't found the clue or the key, and she didn't know what they would do next.

But she was happy too. The merry maids might not be smart or savvy; they might not understand Dyscordia or what was happening in the tunnels, but Kat admired them anyway.

The merry maids watched out for each other and shared everything. They managed to live in harmony in this beautiful world under the ocean, oblivious to the chaos in the deepest reaches of Tutkium all around them They made the best of even the worst of things to hit them. They were truly a family.

No wonder Cornucopia was the destination for this world's feast. It truly was a celebration—of harvest, of plenty, of harmony.

Kat also thought about how Mitsu had finished her rhyme. While she'd asked for the feast and the Gobbler Games to return, Mitsu's rhyme was different. It wasn't only about the food or the games. He, like the merry Marys, knew there were more important things.

I need to try to get along with my siblings more, Kat thought. Her brothers and sisters might tease her a lot, but Kat knew that they loved her. She was lucky to have them, faults and all. The more Kat thought about her family, the more she missed home.

As the Ten-Forty lunged back up into the darkened ocean, its passengers had no Talisman and no clue where to go next. Dyscordia was lurking, seemingly everywhere, always ahead of them. Kat's spirit dropped. Forget about getting home in time for Thanksgiving—Kat wondered if she'd ever get back to Totsville at all.

CHAPTER 10
A TALE OF TWO CITIES: DESTRUCTION AND RESTORATION

Lost in thought about her family, Kat almost didn't notice when another dot on the map started to blink.

When she looked up at Mitsu, his face was wrinkled like a prune.

"You're worried too?" she asked.

"Not worried, Kat McGee," Mitsu said, shaking his head. "Only pensive. Dyscordia has renewed her strength in other chaotic lands in the Tunnels. She knows we are close to finding the Talisman. But you saw how happiness weakened her. It is working, Kat McGee. We must persevere!"

The thought of trying to fend off Malsom and Dyscordia a second time sent a chill down Kat's spine, but the anticipation of finding the key and getting the Ten-Forty back to Totsville filled her with glee again. A glimmer of hope for her beloved Thanksgiving celebrations raced from her toes to her fingers.

"But we didn't get a clue! What will we do?" Despite her worry, Kat smiled at her rhyme. Apparently, the merry maids had made an impression.

The dot on the map blinked more brightly.

Kat leaned closer, squinting to read the two words next to the dot. "Ze-a Mays?" Kat said, trying to sound them out.

Mitsu's eyes widened, getting as large as saucers. "Really? I had not noticed that name on the map before! Are you sure that is what it says?"

As if in answer, beneath the other two phrases, a final clue appeared:

"RESPECT AND HARMONY ARE THE FIRST TWO YOU NOW SEE. TO FIND THE FINAL KEY, YOU MUST RESTORE YOUR FAMILY."

"A clue!" Kat was excited. The map had given them a clue despite their failure! Then the words sank in. "Wait," she looked at Mitsu. Tears trickled down his face, dampening his ever-present smile.

"Are you OK, Mitsu?" Kat reached out and tugged on his arm. "What's wrong? What does it mean? My family isn't even in Tutkium!"

Mitsu shook his head. "No, Kat. I believe the map is talking about my family. I told you how Dyscordia destroyed Tutkium by turning each community against each other. Well, she destroyed my home and our family, the Malimaquiddies, too."

Kat gulped. "Are they . . . dead?"

"They have died in spirit, which is almost worse," Mitsu lamented. "The Malimaquiddies have shut themselves off not just from the rest of Tutkium, but from each other. Many have fled into the caves surrounding Zea Mays, and Dyscordia draws all of her strength from that area now because there is more chaos and fighting and judgment there than anywhere else in Tutkium. That is why her den is so close. That is why I have not been home."

Shocked, Kat looked at Mitsu and back at the map. He was right. Zea Mays was awfully close to Dyscordia's Den.

Which means . . . Kat thought.

As if reading her mind, Mitsu said. "Yes, Kat. If I return to Zea Mays, we will be forced to face Dyscordia. She has taken over the caves very close to my village. We will have to fight her again."

Kat gulped. Goosebumps popped up on her arms at the terrifying prospect. *As the merry maids might say,* she thought, *clue number three is more than a little scary.*

To calm herself down, Kat made a checklist, just like her mom did when she ran errands:

1. Survive trolls and Hole of Hurt. Check.
2. Show respect, get first clue: key ring. Check.
3. Narrowly escape the claws of crazy witch Dyscordia and scary wolf Malsom. Check.
4. Explore and rhyme in wonderful harmony with merry maids. Check.
5. Defeat Dyscordia
6. Find key to the Ten-Forty and return to Totsville before Thanksgiving.

Two tasks left. Less than 24 hours to do them.

As they neared the end of their treasure hunt, Kat was a nervous ball of knots. She couldn't believe she and Mitsu had made it this far, but she also couldn't believe they had to face Dyscordia—again.

Someone was going to lose.

Mitsu's broad, infectious smile, however, had returned. How was he so calm? Without skipping a beat, he maneuvered the Ten-Forty around the jagged rocks spread through the tunnels, which got darker and spookier as they continued.

Finally, they landed, and Kat and Mitsu stepped off the train.

Everything around them was dead, or on the brink of death. Wigwams were falling apart or otherwise destroyed. Crops were burned to the ground. And although Kat saw no people or creatures or any sign of life, she heard horrible screams in the distance, muffled, as if they came from the depths of a dark hole.

"This was your home?" Kat asked Mitsu, horrified.

"My home was never like this. *Zea Mays* means 'Indian corn' in your language. It was a land of life, growth, and *achak*."

Kat wrinkled her nose. "Of what?"

"*Achak*. It means spirit. Every creature and thing in Zea Mays has a unique *achak*. The Tutkim Talisman is the symbol of our *achak*. Without it, the spirit of our people is gone. Now they know only fear, anger, and chaos."

Kat must have looked confused, because Mitsu smiled. Kat was grateful for his patience.

"Your train needs the Talisman," he continued, "not just because it is a key that will make it move and get you home, but because that key symbolizes the *achak* your town of Totsville is missing. It is what you needed to seek, and find, here in Tutkium. The key to your Thanksgiving."

Kat was beginning to understand, "So, Dyscordia didn't just take the key to keep the train from running. She wanted to steal the spirit of Thanksgiving in Totsville! That's why everyone is fighting."

Mitsu smiled. "Yes! Dyscordia does not want a world with this spirit. She will have no power in that world. Once the train is running and we have restored the spirit of Thanksgiving and Potlatch, our people and yours will have the strong minds and open hearts we need to survive—and Dyscordia will cease to exist."

"Where will she go?"

A cold gush of wind blew by, chilling Kat to the bone. "Yes, where will she go?"

The low voice came from the shadows behind them.

Kat whipped around—

And saw her.

Dsycordia, followed closely by Malsom, slunk out of the shadows. Her hands inched along a wall of rock as if it were the only thing keeping her on her feet. She looked sick; her skin was almost translucent, as if she was fading into the darkness around her. In trying to escape Malsom, Kat had only briefly glanced at Dyscordia on the train. Still, she seemed smaller now.

The hatred and fire in her face, however, was stronger and fiercer than ever.

Mitsu's eyes were wide as saucers. Kat looked back and forth between them.

She couldn't run. She couldn't hide. All she could think was . . . *How did I get stuck in the middle?!*

Dyscordia knew she had only one card left to play. She looked at the kid, at her head, darting like a windshield wiper back and forth, back and forth. *Poor little soul*, the Pookcheen-squas thought. *I know exactly what to do.*

She spoke softly. "You know I can help you, Kat McGee. Mitsu wants his silly tunnels back. He's only thinking of his old way of life. He's being selfish. But he can't get you home. I can."

Kat looked at her in astonishment.

"Don't listen to her, Kat McGee," Mitsu warned. "She is trying to pit you against me."

Dyscordia was evil, but could she really get Kat home? Things weren't looking good without the Talisman, and Dyscordia knew where it was. But Kat couldn't trust her. Look at all the destruction she had caused!

"What do you mean?" Kat asked, holding her ground. "You don't want to help me! You and your wolf attacked us! You destroyed our train and took the Tutkium Talisman! Everyone started fighting because of you! You made the rock trolls hate the Malimaquiddies. You keep trying to hurt the merry maids of Cornucopia. You destroyed Zea Mays. Now you're trying to destroy Totsville and steal the spirit of Thanksgiving! Why would I ever believe you?"

Kat was breathless. Instinctively, she took a step back. She wanted to keep her distance.

But Dyscordia was patient, calm. She took a step forward. "Now, now, dear child. You only know half the story. You don't know my side. I did those things to help both of us, your world *and* mine. And I could do more . . . much more."

Mitsu tried to lunge at Dyscordia, but she was too quick. Lightning bolts shot from her steel fingertips. She used her last ounce of strength to hold the old man back. The bolts were weaker than ever before, yet strong enough to keep him still— and quiet.

Mitsu tried to shout, but no sound emerged from his throat.

Dyscordia pointed to her wolf, its teeth bared.

"Guard him, Malsom. If the spell wears off, finish him." The wolf dutifully took his place at Mitsu's feet, ready to pounce.

Dyscordia used the silence to her advantage. This was her chance. "Mitsu and his people don't care about you, Kat," she whispered. "They're just using you to get their stupid Potlatch festival back. You don't need them."

"You're lying. Mitsu has done so much for me," Kat said. Her body quivered from head to toe, but she clenched her fists. She didn't want Dyscordia to see her fear.

"What has he done? He almost had you killed by the rock trolls. And he hadthose silly maids give you some cake? Ha!" Dyscordia laughed maniacally. "Just a ploy to help his beloved Potlatch. Look at him! He can't save you—he can't even save himself! He is helpless, so he is using you."

Kat looked at Mitsu, who was pointing and trying to say something, but Kat couldn't read his lips. Dyscordia couldn't be telling the truth, could she?

Dyscordia felt Kat's doubt and knew her plan was working. Now, she needed to finish the task. What do children love? Dyscordia asked herself. That's when she knew her final play.

The Pookcheensquas took one more step toward the young girl. "Don't you want to know about magic, Kat? Wouldn't you like to fly a train anytime you wanted? You could be the Queen of Tutkium."

Kat closed her eyes. Of course she wanted to learn magic. And she had never been the queen of anything, much less an entire underground kingdom. Her head was spinning.

She looked at Mitsu, trapped. She thought of all the close calls she and Mitsu had survived in Tutkium. She thought of her family. She wanted this all to end—

"I only want Thanksgiving back." Kat said. "I . . . I don't want everyone fighting. That's all."

Dyscordia smiled. "It's not fighting, Kat. It's only a different kind of magic. I can teach it to you."

Kat snapped her head up and looked at Dyscordia. Then she narrowed her eyes, and Wanagamesuk's words rang in her ears: "I am immune to Dyscordia's spells and black magic because I have a strong mind and an open heart."

I knew it! She's trying to trick me! She's trying to do to me what she did to everyone else. She's trying to turn me against Mitsu!

Again Kat looked at Mitsu, stuck in place. His lips were still moving. Impulsively, she followed his gaze. He was looking past Dyscordia, staring into the caves from which the shouts and screams echoed. And he was trying to say one word, over and over again:

Run.

If she thought about it for one more second, she might change her mind.

So she didn't. Taking a deep breath, Kat ran straight into Dyscordia, knocked her over—and kept going.

The fall shattered Dyscordia's lightning hold over Mitsu. Scrambling to regain his balance, he ran into the nearest wigwam.

Dyscordia struggled to her feet. With fire in her eyes, she turned to Malsom. "What are you waiting for? After him! Leave the girl to me. She ran into my den, the little fool. If she doesn't want to play by my rules, I'll finish her off there."

Swoosh!

Whirling her cape around her body, Dyscordia spun in a circle, and disappeared.

Afraid to stop, look back, or turn around, Kat ran through wigwams and darted into the remains of the cornfields. She trampled through charred stalks, throwing them aside with her hands, sprinted out the other end of the field, climbed over a jumble of rocks, and scrambled into a cave up ahead—Dyscordia's Den.

Panting, Kat had to rest. She looked behind her and saw no one. She turned back around and BOOM!

She ran right into Mitsu.

"How did you get here? Are you OK?"

Mitsu was flushed and sweating. "No time. Run, Kat McGee! We must not lose her!"

"Lose her? Isn't she behind me? Wait, why don't we want to lose her?"

Mitsu shook his head and pointed at the cave's entrance. "The Talisman. She will destroy it and both our festivals forever, if we don't stop her. We must hurry!"

With that, Mitsu and Kat ran into the cave. Inside were two domes, leading to two sets of tunnels. How were they supposed to know which one to choose?

"Stop," Mitsu said. "And listen. We will hear the way to go."

The echoes in the different tunnels were indistinguishable. Mitsu closed his eyes. Maybe he had Spidey-senses and could figure out where Dyscordia and Malsom had gone. Kat closed her eyes, too. Maybe she would hear something.

DRIP. DRIP.

The only sound was water trickling down from the walls.

Eyes still closed, Mitsu pointed toward one of the tunnels. "There. Let's go!"

Quickly but carefully, Kat and Mitsu made their way down into the slippery, wet cavern. The dripping echo followed them. Soon, they came to an opening—and heard muffled sounds.

The tunnel opened into a dark, dank room. It was the nucleus of a web of smaller tunnels and caves that extended from it in all directions. Dyscordia stood in the center. She was murmuring quietly, pointing her spindly fingers toward the smaller caves.

"Many Malimaquiddies fled into these caves," Mitsu warned. "She is trying to gather strength from their chaos. We must stop her!"

Kat's mom often told Kat that she needed to think before she spoke, but Kat was furious at Dyscordia for all she had done—to Totsville, to Zea Mays, to the Tunnels of Tutkium. The evil witch had tried to trick her—and Kat was ashamed she had hesitated for even one moment!

Something needed to change.

"Who do you think you are? What did they ever do to you?" Kat shouted.

Dyscordia whipped her cape around and glared at Kat. "Back for more, are you? It's time I teach you a lesson once and for all!" She held out both hands toward Kat, stretching her fingers like she was about to throw her blue and white bolts of pain from the steel tips.

Kat was terrified. She didn't know what was going to happen. Could Dyscordia turn her into a witch . . . or worse?

Raising her arms, Dyscordia started to recite a spell, but Kat closed her eyes and tried to keep a strong mind and an open heart. Memories of all she'd seen over the last two days flashed through her mind: the respect Wanagamesuk had for Mitsu despite the danger of their friendship; Kugu's change of heart when Kat showed respect for her; the merry Marys—how harmoniously they had worked together, and how important family was to them. She thought about all of this, and she smiled.

Because at last, Kat McGee was beginning to understand. She had seen what Thanksgiving was supposed to be about—what Totsville was missing when the train was destroyed—in each of the places they visited. She did need to find the literal key, the Tutkium Talisman, but she knew now that the map was more than a path to that mysterious key. It was a guide, meant to teach Kat the symbols and spirit of Thanksgiving, to show her what Totsville needed to get back:

The importance of respect for people who are not like you.

The importance of gratitude for your family, friends, and the blessings you have.

The importance of harmony and peace in the face of chaos and evil.

And now, at last, Kat knew what she had to do. It was up to her to bring harmony and peace back to Tutkium and back to Totsville.

Taking a deep breath Kat stepped toward Dyscordia. To her surprise, the Pookcheensquas's hands were not shooting lightning bolts at her. In fact, nothing was coming from her fingertips at all. They no longer held blades of steel. Her fingers themselves were almost translucent.

"No, I think someone should teach *you* a lesson!" Kat yelled, surprised at her own boldness.

She stepped forward, but Dyscordia was already up against the wall, with nowhere to go. "Look what you've done!" Kat shouted. "You tricked the trolls to pit them against the Malimaquiddies! You took respect away from them and turned two nations against each other! That isn't how it's supposed to be! The very first Thanksgiving brought two nations together—two very different kinds of people—so they could share their knowledge, their food, and their culture. We have to remember to respect each other even though we're different."

Mitsu looked at Kat and smiled. His proud grin reminded Kat of her parents, of the McGee visit to the Passamaquoddy reservation after their camping trip up north. The Passamaquoddy tribal guide had told them something important, and Kat remembered those wise words now:

"There may always be tension. People have misunderstandings all the time. But that doesn't mean people have to hate each other."

Suddenly, as if summoned by magic, Wanagamesuk and Kugu walked into the cave. Silently, they stood side-by-side behind Kat. She could feel their strength as if it were hers. It helped her find the words Kat wanted to say.

"The *intention* of that first Thanksgiving should never be forgotten."

Wanagamesuk spoke behind her. "When we respect each other, we communicate more."

"And the more we communicate," Kugu added, "the more we understand. Regardless of differences, we can find common ground. We can always strive for peace."

As the rock troll queen spoke, Dyscordia started to shrink toward the floor. To Kat's amazement, she could no longer see Dyscordia's hands or arms—they were fading just like her fingers, which had disappeared. Her cape and dress hung limp.

But her voice hung on.

"You will never get it!" she screeched. "You will never find the Talisman. Tutkium will always be mine!"

But Kat wouldn't stop.

"Thanksgiving is supposed to bring communities together!" As she spoke, Kat thought about the Totsville Thanksgiving Feast and how important it was to so many people.

With every word, Dyscordia's body grew fainter and fainter, fading away bit by bit. Kat couldn't believe her eyes.

Behind her, three merry maids of Cornucopia appeared and joined the group. Kat smiled at them and took a deep breath. She knew she needed to finish what she started.

"The merry maids of Cornucopia show us all what it means to be a family, yet you continuously try to destroy them."

Kat paused. She could only see an outline of what used to be Dyscordia's face. With every second, more of her disappeared. Malsom was behind her, whimpering, pawing at the shape of what used to be his mistress.

"You stole our respect. You made us forget what it's like to be thankful, and you destroyed the harmony in our families," Kat yelled. She stepped forward onto Dyscordia's cape and dress and looked down at the outline of her face.

This was it. In her most confident voice, she yelled, "And now it's time we get them back!"

With all her might and strength, Kat stomped on the cape.

Dyscordia was gone.

CHAPTER 11
THE PILGRIMAGE REDUX

Drip. Drip. The cave was quiet. Without Dyscordia's malicious presence, Malsom looked more like a lost puppy than a treacherous wolf.

Slowly, Kat picked up the cape from the puddle on the cave floor where the witch had stood moments before.

Clang!

A giant key dropped to the floor.

The Tutkium Talisman.

Kat picked it up and looked at Mitsu. "The Talisman! Where was it?"

"It must have been here the whole time. She never let it out of her sight."

Kat looked all around the cave. "But what happened to her?"

"Dyscordia can not exist as a person in places of peace, in places where there are people with strong minds and open hearts. She is now millions of specks of negative energy, floating throughout the universe."

"But will she ever come back?"

"In some form, yes. When you walk into a place where people are fighting, and you feel a sort of tension in the room?

What you feel is a speck of Dyscordia. But as long as we keep the spirit of respect, gratitude, and harmony alive, we will be safe."

Wanagamesuk bowed to Kat. "On behalf of all in the Tunnels of Tutkium, thank you for restoring peace to our land."

The noises coming from the far away caves grew louder. Suddenly, a throng of people—young and old, men and women, some miniature versions of Mitsu, some who looked completely different—streamed out of the caves. Voices swelled from the tunnels, but they were screams of delight, not cries of fear or shouts of anger. Mitsu ran to hug his family. Everyone pointed at Kat, cheering and clapping, celebrating being free at long last of Dyscordia and her evil charms.

The merry Marys put a homemade leash around Malsom's neck, gave him a miniature pie treat, and then the throng of happy Tutkiumites all headed out of the cave together.

As they left, Kat exclaimed, "I can't believe it! Did I do that?! It all happened so fast!"

Mitsu laughed, "You did it! You showed Dyscordia the *achak* of Thanksgiving and our Potlatch. Now you will truly be able to celebrate! And we will be able to celebrate with you!"

"Oh no!" Kat had forgotten about the time crunch. "We have to get out of here! Can I make it back to Totsville by Thanksgiving? Will the Talisman work and repair the Ten-Forty!"

"Well, my young *espons*, there is only one way to find out!"

Mitsu sat in his chair at the controls, but for the first time, the map did not light up. The controls were dark. Nothing moved, whirred, or stirred.

Wrinkling his brow in confusion, Mitsu pushed every button, turned every knob, and pulled every lever.

Still nothing.

"I was afraid of this," Mitsu said. "You are the only person who can get the Ten-Forty out of Tutkium. It is your turn at the controls now. I must leave."

Kat shook her head nervously. "But I need you! The map isn't flashing, and I can't run the train alone! How will I ever find my way?"

Mitsu laughed. "You will not be alone. SJ will help guide you."

"The voice in the train?" Kat asked, perplexed. "Whose voice is it? Who is SJ?"

Mitsu's eyebrows shot up on his forehead. "You do not know? Your gram did not tell you? SJ is Sarah Josepha Hale, of course. Gram introduced me to her when she came to Tutkium on the Ten-Forty! SJ will be with you."

Kat's mouth dropped to the floor. "Sarah Hale? The Sarah Hale that convinced President Lincoln to make Thanksgiving a holiday? That's whose voice I've been hearing this entire time?"

Mitsu nodded, smiling warmly at her. "Her spirit, and voice, are a part of the Ten-Forty, always."

"You must go, young *espons*. Thank you. May you always keep your strong *achak*."

Kat reached over and gave Mitsu a huge bear hug. Mitsu squeezed her back, and Kat felt his warmth and love. For the first time in a while, she felt like she was going to be OK.

Determined, Kat climbed into the conductor's chair and slid the Tutkium Talisman into the Ten-Forty's throttle. The controls lit up. The engine whirred. The Ten-Forty roared to life.

Mitsu stepped off the train into Zea Mays. As soon as the Talisman was back in its place, the ground of Zea Mays transformed from black dirt and rock to green grass and fertile fields. The Malimaquiddies were already getting to work patching and repairing their wigwams.

Kat smiled. Zea Mays was going to be OK, too.

As if reading her mind, Mitsu yelled. "*Woliwon*, Kat McGee! We will miss you!"

A merry Mary exclaimed, "The train will run! It's been so much fun! Kat McGee, you have won!"

Through the window of the train, Kat waved goodbye, again, to her new friends. But as she buckled her seatbelt, a wave of concern hit her.

Tomorrow was Thanksgiving! Even if she did make it back to Totsville, the council had no way of going on the pilgrimage. There wouldn't be enough food for the feast!

Then Kat remembered the lessons of her adventure. If the people of Totsville stopped fighting, it didn't matter how much food they had or what they did on the holiday. As long as they were together as families, and as a community, it would be a perfect Thanksgiving.

She just hoped that things had returned to normal in Totsville, the way they had in the Tunnels of Tutkium.

Taking a deep breath, Kat looked out the window. The Ten-Forty already looked more resplendent. The key was working! It was restoring the train's *achak*. Her eyes scanned the control board. Would Sarah Hale's voice really help her find her way home? So far, she'd heard nothing.

Kat yawned, and her whole body ached with exhaustion. Except for the nap she had taken upon leaving Trolltropolis, she hadn't slept in three days!

That's when she heard the familiar woman's voice.

"All aboard! Welcome to the Ten-Forty. Our final destination will be Totsville, Maine. Please enjoy your trip."

Kat sighed with relief. Her shoulders lightened like a huge weight had been lifted from them. Her eyelids sagged heavily. It felt like someone was pulling them closed. But she didn't fret.

She was going home.

Kat had the strangest dream.

She dreamed the Ten-Forty flew out of the tunnels and high up into the sky—so high that Kat could no longer see the ground. Stars twinkled brightly all around them.

Then she dreamed that the Town Council was in the Ten-Forty with her. The council members were laughing and talking—about the pilgrimage, about how excited they were to get back to Totsville.

Sarah Hale's voice announced the first stop: Turkey Township. The train stopped, and the mayor picked up a load of turkeys. The man who delivered them had a thin face and squinty eyes. His arm muscles were so defined that his biceps and shoulders looked like rocks. But he wasn't intimidating. He was kind and interested in the Turkey Train's journey.

"You tell everyone in Totsville to have a Happy Thanksgiving from all of us in Turkey Township," he said. "Hope to see you again before next year!"

Next, the train stopped in Pie Parish. The sweet Sweeney sisters knew the council was in a hurry, so in addition to delivering their usual fresh, mouth-watering pies, they dropped off shellfish from Oceanview. The sisters giggled and laughed with the council about their travels, seeming impossibly merry.

As the train pulled out of the station, the Sweeney sisters waved goodbye and yelled, "We love your visits—come again soon! We'll have a good time; maybe sing a tune!"

The final stop was in Corn County. Recently, Native American tribes all over the county had suffered a big storm. Now, everyone in town was picking up debris and helping each other repair fences, fix windows in storefronts, and replace doors on houses.

Back on the train, Mayor Little said, "I love the people in Corn County. It was so nice of them to bring us fresh vegetables from Farmville. They really know how to help others, even after that terrible storm trashed their town!"

Kat couldn't believe she was on the pilgrimage, meeting all these wonderful people, seeing all these amazing things. Best of all, they were going to roll into Town Square just in the nick of time.

CHAPTER 12
A TOTSVILLE THANKSGIVING

Kat awoke. Shivering, she lifted her head and looked around.

Photos of the Ten-Forty lined the walls. Newspaper clippings and magazine articles were spread on display tables.

She was in the back of the Ten-Forty. But it was a museum again—not a flying magical train.

Someone knocked on the door.

"You're going to miss the ceremony, Miss McGee," a voice said from outside. "I'm afraid I have to open up the Ten-Forty now. People are starting to arrive."

Wait a minute. Kat jumped up. *How did I get here?! Arrive for what?*

She ran to the door and swung it open. Herman smiled up at her. Kat looked around. Everyone in Totsville was gathering in Town Square near the restored Ten-Forty.

"When did I get back?" Kat asked Herman. "Where's Mitsu?" Belatedly, she glanced down at her feet. Her shell shoes were gone.

Herman looked confused. "Get back? Miss McGee, you've been here for hours. You and your gram. She told me you had fallen asleep and asked me to keep a look out while she went home and got the rest of your family. I shouldn't have allowed it, but your gram sweet-talked. Promised me some Turkey Day Tamales in fact. They should be back any minute!"

"So the Ten-Forty made it out of the tunnels in one piece? Wowzas! I'm just sorry we didn't make it back in time for the Town Council to go on the pilgrimage!"

Shaking his head in bemusement, Herman helped Kat down the steps. "I'm not sure what you're talking about Miss McGee, but the council is back on schedule. They had to cut the trip a little short, but those sweet sisters up in Pie Parish helped out by picking up the load in Oceanview, and the folks in Corn County delivered the rest of the vegetables from Farmville. Now everyone's back and getting ready for the presentation!"

Kat jumped up and down, unable to contain her excitement. "So we're having the Thanksgiving Feast? And the Gobbler Games?"

Herman looked at Kat strangely. "Are you feeling alright, Miss McGee? Of course we're having the feast and the games. It wouldn't be Totsville without them. But you know that, little lady!"

That's when Kat's family rounded the corner, wearing full Troubadour regalia. Thanking Herman, Kat rushed over to hug her parents.

"Happy Thanksgiving! I'm so happy to see you!" Kat cried, flinging her arms around her mom.

Polly handed Kat a Troubadour shirt. "Gram told me to bring this for you, since we won't have time to go home before the feast."

Kat smiled, took the shirt, and hugged Polly tightly. "Thank you so much! That's really sweet of you." She wondered if Gram was far behind. She could hardly wait to talk to her!

Polly looked at Kat. "What's wrong with *you*?"

Kat looked at her family and smiled. "Absolutely nothing, Polly. I couldn't be happier."

Oh, what a day it was!

The Thanksgiving Feast was the best ever. Hannah liked Mrs. Vui's eggrolls the most, but Kat's highlights were Mayor Little's turkey, the Mehtas' curried stuffing, and Gram's Turkey Day Tamales, of course. However, this year, Kat didn't stuff herself like a turkey; she wanted to have plenty of energy to put her best foot forward at the Gobbler Games.

To top it all off, Anjali Mehta came over and sat with Kat for a while. She told Kat how her mother made the curried stuffing. It was a family secret, but Kat promised not to tell.

Anjeli had never talked to Kat before. Kat asked a lot of questions about her family, what they did at Thanksgiving, and what other traditions they had. The answers were fascinating. Anjeli even invited her over to hang out after the Gobbler Games. It seemed that Kat had a new friend!

After Thanksgiving, Kat was a Gobbler Games superstar. Well, by Kat McGee standards. She didn't drop the baton (as she regularly did in practice) during her leg of the relay race, and she didn't fall during the game of tug of war. She got a little tripped up in the obstacle course, but surprisingly, her family

didn't give her a hard time. Instead, they patted Kat on the back and said she'd done a good job.

On the way home, Abe said, "Way to go, Kat. You didn't totally screw up."

Kat smiled. Any compliment from Abe was huge.

But her mind was scrambling. *What is going on? Did I dream everything? Was the Ten-Forty and Mitsu and Dyscordia all a crazy, frightening, exciting, amazing fantasy?* No one in her family seemed to have noticed she was gone. And she tried and tried to pull Gram aside and talk to her about the adventure alone, but someone always interrupted, or Gram was needed elsewhere.

That night, at the final campfire, with the Ten-Forty glowing in the firelight behind him, Mayor Little stood to announce the results of the Gobbler Games.

"We will be giving two awards this year," the mayor said. "The first goes to the team that narrowly triumphed. It was the closest tally in Gobbler Games history, but for the first time in nine years, we have a new champion. Congratulations to the Troubadours!"

They'd done it! The Troubadours had won in spite of Kat's mediocre performance. The curse was broken! Kat's siblings hugged her tightly. Not the obligatory hugs the McGees forced on their children, but a real, genuine hug.

All around them, the many Troubadour families jumped up and down, congratulating each other. But this year, they also congratulated the Tuckahoes. And instead of groans, the Tuckahoes hollered and cheered as loudly as the Troubadours—everyone celebrated!

Kat didn't think the night could get any better, but it did.

"The Troubadours will get their names on the Hale Halo, which, as always, will be displayed on the Ten-Forty," the mayor continued. "But this year, I would also like to make a special dedication to someone who's recently taught me a lot about Thanksgiving. We had a rough week here in Totsville, but the day and week surrounding Thanksgiving isn't only about the amazing feast and wonderful games. The meaning behind these events—respect, gratitude, and harmony—are what we as a nation, a town, and as families are lucky enough to celebrate each and every year."

Whispers spread throughout the crowd.

Kat looked around. *Wait a minute. Does the mayor know about my adventure? How . . . what . . . ?*

"I'm told she, or he, wants to remain anonymous, that this person doesn't want us all to know the big part she or he played in restoring the Ten-Forty in time for our pilgrimage," The mayor said. "But as a thank you to that person, I would like to put a new plaque on the Ten-Forty. I consulted with some of our neighboring Native American elders so I could find the perfect word for this award."

The crowd murmured. Who could it be? What kind of award?

Mayor Little continued, "So I hope whoever it is sees it someday and smiles. I present the first-ever Spirit of Thanksgiving Achak plaque. It will always have a place in Totsville on the Ten-Forty. May it inspire us all to seek respect, to remember gratitude, and to find harmony!"

The townspeople applauded and whooped. And Kat's heart melted. Kat glanced around at her brothers and sisters and spotted Gram's glowing face. Keeping her head down to hide her giant smile, Kat crawled over to her grandmother. They looked at each other and smiled.

"Where'd you learn how to cook your Turkey Day Tamales, Gram?" Kat asked. "Perhaps Mitsu taught you the recipe in the Tunnels of Tutkium?"

Gram turned to Kat with a twinkle in her eye. "A chef can't tell her secrets, Kool Kat."

But Kat had a feeling Gram knew all about her adventures in Tutkium. She was sure of it. Kat knew it wasn't a dream.

As she sat back and enjoyed the rest of the evening with her family, Kat thought of Mitsu, looked at her Gram, and whispered, "*Woliwon*, Gram. *Woliwon*."

***

Later that night, alone in her room, Kat slowly unrolled the magic map Gram had given her less than a week earlier. Nothing lit up. The stars were only dots on the page. The trail still connected the dots, but the X in the corner seemed much smaller and more faded. Squinting, Kat focused on the words scattered over the page.

"Trolltropolis," she read, whispering the words in the dark. "Merry Maids of Cornucopia. Zea Mays. Dyscordia's Den."

Kat marveled at the places she had seen and the people she had met. She wished for a moment that she could share it with her family and all the people of Totsville—maybe even get a little recognition, let people know that the Achak plaque belonged to her.

Gus would have loved Mitsu's magic. Polly would have gone nuts trying to find the missing part of the train. Even Hannah would have gotten a kick out of the merry Marys. And her parents would have been so proud to see Kat learning about respect, gratitude, and family.

Thanksgiving was right, Kat thought. She was thankful for a lot of things: Gram and the rest of her family; the people

of Totsville; the respect she saw between her neighbors again. Though she was happy about her performance at the games, she had learned why the holiday wasn't just about the delicious feast or the thrill of victory.

It was then that Kat realized she didn't want recognition. She didn't need to share her story with her family.

Kat slumped back on her beanbag in her room on the corner of the fourth floor, safe in Totsville, home with her family, and happy. Her brothers and sisters all had something special, a skill or hobby or sport at which they excelled. She'd always been sure she didn't have a "thing", and had feared that she might never have one. As she closed her eyes and drifted to sleep, she realized now she had her "thing."

That thing was holidays. And that was enough.

EPILOGUE

"Well?" Gram asked. "What do you think?"

Dolce and Mitsu looked at Kat, sound asleep on her beanbag. Gently, Venus and Mother Nature placed a blanket over her.

"I think she is ready!" Mitsu said, always excited. He was not very good at whispering.

Sadie, finger to her lips, shushed him. To Gram, she murmured, "She has many tests and trials ahead of her. And much to learn."

"True." Gram nodded. "But you will all help her. We all will help her, too."

Dolce smiled. "We'll need to make sure she doesn't remember this journey, or you, Mitsu—until the time is right. This kind of secret is a big responsibility. And it could be years before she is finished."

Gram nodded. "Agreed. You take care of her memory, Dolce."

Peering through the window, Liberty added, "She won't be able to join us until the job is done. And we never know when threats or dangers will appear."

"Of course, Liberty. But that's the adventure of it all, is it not? Let's just take them one at a time," Gram said. "One at a time."

THE END . . . for now.

ACKNOWLEDGMENTS

I'd like to thank the village that makes up Team Kat: Carey Albertine and Saira Rao at the helm, Nick Guarracino for his time and incredible vision, Kati Robins for her challenging and fun guides, Genevieve Gagne-Hawes for continuing to lend her invaluable perspective and help, and Shannon Miller for coming aboard and spreading the Kat love. Thanks to the students, teachers, librarians, and parents who are giving Kat a chance and joining the adventure. Thanks to each Riddick, Kirkwood, Glaze, Herring, and Talley piece of my familial pie for being the supportive, crazy, fun, strange, sweet, salty, and most important centerpiece to my Thanksgiving (and every) holiday table. And thanks to David—through my many stumbles, bumps, and tears on this journey—for always picking me up and helping me find my smile. I am overflowing with joy, hope, and gratitude for our newest and greatest adventure yet—ready or not, here we come.

Proverbs 3:5,6

ABOUT THE AUTHOR

Kristin Riddick, like Kat, never met an adventure she didn't like. She has acted in commercials, sitcoms, webisodes, and her husband's road trip movies. Her voice can be heard on television and in films, but you will never know it is hers so it seems very mysterious. She teaches Pilates and spinning to stay sane, and because she thinks it puts people in better moods. Kristin is a native of Corpus Christi, Texas, and a graduate of The University of Virginia. She currently divides her time between Los Angeles and Austin with her husband, and they will soon be starting the greatest adventure of all—parenthood.

Connect with Kristin
www.kristinriddick.com
www.facebook.com/AKatMcgeeAdventure
twitter: @katmcgeebooks

Other Books in the Kat McGee series:
Kat McGee and the School of Christmas Spirit
Kat McGee and the Halloween Costume Caper
Kat McGee Saves America

Kat McGee and the Thanksgiving Turkey Train
By Kristin Riddick

CHAPTER 1: The Totsville Feast and Gobbler Games

Vocabulary Words: agony, imposed, regimens, faint, rigorous, anticipation, bickering, prowess, quintessential, mediocre, quantify, pilgrimage

Discussion Questions:

1. In the Prologue, there is a special message for you. Who is the message from?

_____

In your own words, explain what it says?

_____

_____

_____

2. What are the Gobbler Games? _____

_____

_____

_____

3. While training for the Gobbler Games, Kat's siblings teased her for finishing in last place. Have you ever been teased for finishing last, or not being good at something? If so, what did you get teased for and how did it make you feel?

_____

_____

_____

4. What are 5 things Kat likes about this time of year?

    1. _____

    2. _____

    3. _____

    4. _____

    5. _____

5. Explain why Kat doesn't have a lot of friends.

_____

_____

_____

6. What is Kat's only major interest?

_____

7. What is the Totsville Ten-Forty?

_____

_____

8. Why does Kat believe that she has cursed the Troubadours?

_____

Activities:

Create a character log for Kat. Include information about her background and family members, adjectives that describe her physical appearance and personality, her likes and dislikes, and her strengths and weaknesses. As you read, continue to add information and details to your log.

Masala turkey and curried stuffing, a variety of oyster dishes, homemade eggrolls, and sauerkraut; Kat loved tasting the dishes that her friends from different cultures would bring to the feast. As a class, create your own collection of Thanksgiving recipes. Have each student contribute one recipe that represents the culture of his or her origin.

Along the trail of the Ten-Forty, the council stopped to gather food and supplies from all over Maine for their feast. Research your state to identify local products you could collect to contribute to your feast. Identify the product and its location.

For the Gobbler Games, the entire town of Totsville divided into two tribes, the Troubadours and the Tuckahoes. Define each of these terms and create an argument explaining why the author chose them to identify the opposing teams in Totsville.

CHAPTER 2: Trouble in Totsville

Vocabulary Words: demolished, reverie, reenactments, luxuriously, restored, epicenter, emblem, relic, bygone, disjointed, remnants, glumly, perpetrators, proposed, adorned, chided, sabotage, profanity

Discussion Questions:

1. Why was the Ten-Forty forced to retire?
_____

_____

2. What 3 nicknames did the Ten-Forty collect over the years?

   1. _____

   2. _____

   3. _____

3. Why have the Gobbler Games and Thanksgiving feast been postponed? _____

_____

_____

4. *Tension and accusations spread like wildfire through every home and family.* What does this sentence mean?

_____

_____

5. At the end of the chapter, someone rings Kat's doorbell. Who do you think is at the door?

_____

Activities:

The Totsville Ten-Forty used to be the most famous train in all of Maine. People from as far away as Florida and California came to Totsville to see it. On a map, calculate the distance between Florida and Maine, and California and Maine.

Using the information in this chapter, create a PowerPoint Presentation explaining and illustrating the history and establishment of Totsville. Include three comparisons between the settlement of Totsville and of your home town.

Gone was the restored, shiny, beautiful relic of a bygone era that had welcomed hundreds of tourists and guests. Replacing it were disjointed pieces of steel, wood, and metal that looked more like a Lego project gone bad than a train. Using Legos, create a replica of what you imagine the restored, shiny Ten-Forty looked like before it was ruined.

Compare and contrast the spirit of the Gobbler Games in years prior to the destruction of the Ten-Forty, and the current spirit of the Games. Include specific examples.

Kristin Riddick

Kat McGee and The Thanksgiving Turkey Train

CHAPTER 3: A Magical Map

Vocabulary List: lackluster, precisely, provoked, loot, reassurance, dumbstruck, receptacle, aficionada

Discussion Questions:

1. Who arrives at Kat's door?
___

2. How did Gram know that something was terribly wrong?
___
___

3. *Kat couldn't put her finger on what made the relationship with her grandmother so special, but it was as if they knew a secret language no one else understood.* Explain the meaning of this sentence.
___
___

4. What gift did Kat receive from Gram?
___

5. What two sentences appear next to the X?
___

6. What is the code?
___

7. What do you think the code means? _____

_____

_____

8. Why did Kat decide not to ask for help from her siblings?

_____

_____

Activities:

Create a character log for Gram. Include information about her background and family members, adjectives that describe her physical appearance and personality, her likes and dislikes, and her strengths and weaknesses. As you read, continue to add information and details to your log.

Crack the code! Using the details in this chapter, create your own Magical Map just like the one Gram gave to Kat. On the back, record the secret code and collect clues as you continue reading to see if you can solve the mystery of the Ten-Forty before Kat does.

Find a Turkey Tamale recipe in a cookbook or on the Internet, and with your family, make your own to enjoy Kat's favorite Thanksgiving menu item.

Kat McGee and The Thanksgiving Turkey Train

CHAPTER 4: The Resurrection of the Ten-Forty

Vocabulary List: resurrection, mischievous, tenure, demise, predicament, emphasized, eerily, distraught, cryptically, alter, deflated, morphed

Discussion Questions:

1. Why do you think Kat didn't want to lie to Gram?
_____
_____

2. When did the vandals strike the Ten-Forty?
_____
_____

3. What does Gram say to Kat as she exits the train to keep Herman company? _____
_____

4. In your own words, describe what happens to Kat on the train after Gram leaves._____
_____
_____
_____

5. Kat thinks she's cracked the code. What does she think the symbols stand for? _____

_____

_____

6. What makes Kat McGee faint for the first time in her nine-year-old life? _____

_____

_____

7. What do you predict will happen next? _____

_____

_____

_____

_____

_____

Activities:

Using the details in this chapter, draw a picture of the curvy woman with indigo hands that keeps appearing in Kat's mind.

Create your own code. Replace the letters of the alphabet with symbols. Use those symbols to write a message to a friend, and see if they can crack the code to find the meaning of your message.

In Ancient Egypt people communicated using a code. They wrote using symbols, or picture words, called Hieroglyphics. Use the Internet to find answers to the following questions, and share your findings with your class.

- What does the word Hieroglyph mean?
- How do we know how to read Hieroglyphics?
- What did Ancient Egyptians write on, and what did they write with?
- How many Hieroglyphs are there?
- Find a Hieroglyphic Alphabet Translator, and discover your name written in Hieroglyphics.

CHAPTER 5: Into the Tunnels of Tutkium

Vocabulary List: disheveled, paraphernalia, dissipate, reticence, defensively, perplexed, astounded, figurative, cavernous, crimson, crevices, summoned

Discussion Questions:

1. After the Ten-Forty arrives, a new code appears next to the X. What does the new code say? _____

2. Where did Kat land? _____

_____

3. Who had come to help Kat? _____

4. Describe Tutkium. _____

_____

_____

5. What does Mitsu teach Kat about her Gram? _____

_____

6. What clue does Mitsu discover about what Kat needs to find to fix the Ten-Forty? _____

_____

6. Who is Malsom?

_____

And, to whom do you think Malsom belongs?

_____

Activities:

Mitsu teaches Kat many new Native American words. Create a glossary and record the meaning of all of the Native American words that Mitsu introduces to Kat.

At the end of this chapter, a new character is introduced. Use the descriptive language to illustrate a picture of her.

CHAPTER 6: The Pookcheensquas's Pursuit

Vocabulary List: trickery, insecure, inflicted, conveyed, daunting, gargantuan, affirmative

Discussion Questions:

1. What keeps Dyscordia alive?_____

2. How did Dyscordia destroy Tutkium? _____

_____

_____

3. What must Kat and Mitsu do to save Totsville and defeat Dyscordia? _____

_____

_____

4. What is the Talisman?_____

5. In your own words, explain what Mitsu means when he says, *You do not give yourself enough credit, Kat McGee! You have to believe in yourself as a person who embodies and spreads the qualities of respect and peace. And then you will. It may be the only way to save your world and mine!* _____

_____

_____

_____

_____

_____

Activities:

Using the information in this chapter, create a T-chart listing the similarities between the demise of Tutkium and what is currently happening in Totsville.

Kat McGee and The Thanksgiving Turkey Train

CHAPTER 7: The Trolls of Intolerance

Vocabulary List: intolerance, maliciously, flanked, disconcerting, suppress, enveloped, blunt, literally, reconcile, respectful, vehement, jeers, aptly, emanated, falter, impulsively

Discussion Questions:

1. Who is Kat and Mitsu's only ally in Trolltopolis?
_____
2. Who is Kugu?_____

3. Kat hates talking to adults. Do you? Explain. _____
_____
_____

4. In your own words, explain what Wanagamesuk means when he says, *I do not believe in hurting other people because they are different from me. I have deep respect for Mitsu and his people, just as he does for me. That he looks and speaks and eats in ways that I think strange makes no difference.*
_____
_____
_____
_____

5. Why is Wanagamesuk immune to Dyscordia's spells and black magic? _____

_____

6. What type of people does Dyscordia poison? _____

_____

7. What important lesson did Kat's mother teach her about the differences between families in Totsville? _____

_____

_____

8. Why did Mitsu choose to show Kugu respect, *even when being respectful was the hardest thing to do?* _____

_____

_____

_____

9. What does Kugu give Kat to help her find the Talisman? __

_____

Kat McGee and The Thanksgiving Turkey Train

Activities:

Mitsu said, *I think in terms of your miles, it is 3958.8 from the Earth's surface to its center. Our world is somewhere in the middle.* Create a digital model, or drawing, of the Earth's core and the mileage from its surface to the center. Be sure to label the surface, the center, and Kat and Mitsu's location when they land at the beginning of this chapter.

With a partner, create a Venn diagram showing the similarities and differences between the conflicts of the first settlers and the Native Americans, and those of the rock trolls and humans in Trolltopolis.

CHAPTER 8: Close Encounters of the Dyscordia Kind

Vocabulary List: vigorously, cornucopia, immune, ferociously, instinctively, devour, undaunted, disintegrated

Discussion Questions:

1. What is the new clue that Kat receives?
_____
_____

What do you think it means? _____
_____

2. Explain the Greek mythology of the word *cornucopia*.
_____
_____
_____

3. What weapon did Mitsu and Kat use to defend themselves against Dyscordia and Malsom's evil attacks?
_____

Kat McGee and The Thanksgiving Turkey Train

Activities:

In this chapter, Kat and Mitsu use kindness to defeat evil. Think about our world today, and list three ways in which YOU can use kindness to defeat evil in your everyday lives.

1. _____

   _____

2. _____

   _____

3. _____

   _____

CHAPTER 9: The Merry Maids of Cornucopia

Vocabulary List: protest, myriad, incredulous, haste, contrary, tarry, unison, entranced, bleak, incensing, exasperated, deluge, savvy

Discussion Questions:

1. At the beginning of this chapter, where does the Ten-Forty land? Be specific.

_____

_____

2. What do you notice about how the merry Marys speak?

_____

_____

3. Who did Kat's sister, Hannah dress-up as for Halloween, and why?_____

_____

4. Why did Kat think the Marys were so lucky? _____

_____

5. What does Mitsu mean when he says, *That is the million-dollar question?*

_____

6. Why did Kat admire the Marys so much?

_____

_____

_____

Activities:

With a partner, create a list of all of the rhyming words in this chapter. See how many you can find!

Choose your favorite part of Kat's adventure, so far. Create a rhyme, rap, or song that describes what happens and explains why it is your favorite. Present it to your class.

CHAPTER 10: A Tale of Two Cities: Destruction and Resurrection

Vocabulary List: pensive, persevere, judgment, prospect, cease, translucent, astonishment, emerged, dutifully, ploy, indistinguishable, tension, summoned

Discussion Questions:

1. What is the final clue that Kat receives?
_____
_____

What do you think it means?
_____
_____

2. Why hasn't Mitsu gone home? _____
_____
_____

3. What are the two tasks Kat has left?

    1. _____

    2. _____

4. What is the *achak* of Totsville? _____

5. Why is Dyscordia trying to pit Kat against Mitsu?
_____

_____

Have you ever had someone try to pit you against another? Explain. _____

_____

_____

6. Why is Kat immune to Dyscordia's spell?
_____

_____

7. What is the map trying to show Kat about what Totsville needs to get back?

_____

_____

_____

_____

8. What lesson did Kat teach Dyscordia?
_____
_____
_____

9. What were the wise words spoken by the Passamaquoddy tribal guide?
_____
_____

10. What was the intention of the first Thanksgiving, and why must it never be forgotten? _____
_____
_____
_____
_____
_____

Kat McGee and The Thanksgiving Turkey Train

Activities:

Out of desperation, Dyscordia tries to convince Kat that she is trying to help her get home. In what other stories that you've read does the villain try to lure the protagonist in the same way?

Pretend that you are the author of this story. Now that Dyscordia is gone, write what will happen next to Kat McGee, Mitsu and the rest of Tutkium and Totsville.

_____
_____
_____
_____
_____
_____
_____
_____
_____
_____
_____

Kristin Riddick

CHAPTER 11: The Pilgrimage Redux

Vocabulary List: treacherous, resplendent, intimidating

Discussion Questions:

1. What happened to Dyscordia, and will she ever come back?

_____

_____

What must Kat, Mitsu, and the others do to stay safe from Dyscordia? _____

_____

2. Who is SJ? _____

_____

3. As Kat was worrying about having enough food for the feast, she remembered the lessons of her adventure. What was most important to Kat? _____

_____

Activities:

On the voyage home, Kat rests her eyes and has a strange dream about being on the Ten-Forty with the town Council, collecting food for the feast. List as many similarities as you can find between this dream Kat has and her adventure in Tutkium?

Kristin Riddick

Kat McGee and The Thanksgiving Turkey Train

CHAPTER 12: A Totsville Thanksgiving

Vocabulary List: belatedly, bemusement, regalia, obligatory, marveled, obligatory

Discussion Questions:

1. What were Kat's favorite dishes at the Thanksgiving feast?

    1. _____

    2. _____

    3. _____

2. Why didn't Kat stuff herself like a turkey at the feast?

_____

3. What positive things came out of Kat and Anjeli talking together for the very first time at the feast?

_____

4. What new plaque did Mayor Little want to put up in the Ten-Forty? _____

_____

5. What did Kat realize was her special "thing"?

_____

6. In the Epilogue, Mitsu says, *I think she is ready!* What do you think Kat is ready for? And, are you excited to join her?

_____

_____

_____

Activities:

As a class, have your own Thanksgiving feast, and have everyone bring a dish that is representative of their heritage. Learn about and celebrate each other's differences with a strong mind and an open heart. Afterwards, participate in your own Gobbler Games. Decide together what the games will be, and play them with respect, harmony, and gratitude.

For more educational and character-building activities, visit beanoblekid.org

Made in the USA
Charleston, SC
31 October 2015